Edward Thomson

Selected Essays

Edward Thomson

Selected Essays

ISBN/EAN: 9783337277932

Printed in Europe, USA, Canada, Australia, Japan

Cover: Foto ©Andreas Hilbeck / pixelio.de

More available books at **www.hansebooks.com**

SELECTED ESSAYS.

BY

EDWARD THOMSON, D. D., LL. D.,

Late a Bishop of the Methodist Episcopal Church.

Published for the Epworth League.

CRANSTON & CURTS: CINCINNATI, CHICAGO, ST. LOUIS.

HUNT & EATON: NEW YORK.

1893.

CONTENTS.

THE education developed in these pages is not one that displays a mock morality and a false faith, but one in which the religion of the Bible is made to assume its true place as the foundation-stone. Everywhere does the author recognize the importance of combining religious culture with general education, in order that the world may be saved from the curse of unsanctified knowledge.

The author of these essays is said to be of the same family stock as James Thomson, the poet of the "Seasons." What Lord Littleton said of the poet, we believe may be said with equal propriety of the essayist—that his writings contain

"No line which, dying, he could wish to blot."

General Education.

THE history of education may be divided into four periods. The first, commencing with the fall of man and extending to the Deluge, comprehends a term of two thousand years, and may be denominated the patriarchal. It is probable that, in this period, the whole race was in a semi-barbarous condition; they wandered in deserts and forests, depending upon fishing and the chase for subsistence, and consuming all their time and expending all their energies in procuring the necessaries of life. They had no agriculture, commerce, navigation, arts, or science worthy of the name. Their wars were collisions of brute force; their governments were of the simpiest kind, growing, in most instances, out of the influence of aged patriarchs or veteran chiefs; their arts were few and rude; their sciences consisted of a few phenomena, perverted to superstitious purposes; their religion, though based upon important revelations, was obscured, if not obliterated, by vain imaginations. The little knowledge which they possessed was transmitted only by tradition, as they had no written language. Their wealth was poverty, their courage fe rocity, their wisdom superstition, their religion idolatry. God was the only teacher, and it was but now and then that he opened heaven and let down a truth upon them. Their wickedness hung an impenetrable cloud over them, and the few beams that darted through it from the skies were soon absorbed and lost in prevailing

5

errors. There was, however, at all times, one luminous spot on earth, though often bound by a circle a few feet in diameter. Enoch, Nimrod, Noah, and kindred worthies, manifested vigorous intellect. The history of antediluvian ages is nearly lost; nor need we deplore the obscurity which rests over that distant period, since we know that it had no influence upon postdiluvian times, and that, if the vail could be removed, we could obtain no valuable information.

After the Deluge, the human mind manifested increased activity. Less than two hundred years subsequent to that event, Nimrod, or Belus, laid the foundations of Babylon, and Ashur built Nineveh, which became the capital of the Assyrian empire. Not long posterior, the Egyptian empire was founded by Menes, or Mizraim.

A period of energy, and effort, and light ensued, comprehending the history of the palmy days of Egypt, Greece, and Rome, and embracing a period of more than two thousand years. The first and perhaps the greatest development of human intellect, was in the valley of the Nile. Egypt attained an elevation in science, arts, and song, to which the world must look up for ages to come. The pyramids, temples, obelisks, columns, and colossal statues at Thebes, still remain—having resisted the desolations of time for many successive centuries—and attest the power, the perseverance, and the skill of Egyptian artisans. The shriveled mummy, torn from the emboweled catacomb, and transported to a distant shore, to gratify the eye of vain and eager curiosity, reminds us that arts, of which we are ignorant, were known in early ages to Egypt. Pompey's Pillar, Cleopatra's Needles, and the forests of columns, and piles of ruins that are scattered all along the "city of the Dead," bear ample attestation to the ancient glory of Alexandria.

It is reasonable to suppose that when mankind passed from the migratory to the settled condition, the adjustment of the boundaries of their possessions would be an object of attention. Accordingly, we find that geometry is an ancient science; and although its methods, in early ages, were coarse, it nevertheless subserved the most valuable purposes.

To what extent the natural sciences were cultivated we are at a loss to conceive; but we have sufficient ground to conjecture, that the external character of fossils, the structure of the earth, the nature of vegetables, and the history of animals, were by no means over-looked by the philosophers of Egypt.

The more important phenomena of the heavens were observed in a very early age; and although no satisfactory manner of accounting for them was devised till a later period, yet the astronomical knowledge of antiquity was as accurate, if not as extensive, as widely diffused, though not as philosophical, as that of the nineteenth century of the Christian era. The phases of the moon, the precession of the equinoxes, the differences between solar and sidereal time were all familiarly known to ancient Egypt. The zodiac was divided into signs by a process simple and ingenious, and requiring a perseverance worthy of the highest reward. So common was astronomical knowledge in those early ages, that we have reason to suppose almost every distinguished individual had a horoscope, and that the zodiacs found in the ruins of Estne and Dendara are specimens of that instrument. The true system of astronomy, supposed by many to be the achievement of modern science, was taught by Pythagoras five hundred and ninety years prior to the Christian era, and was probably derived by him from Æunophis, an Egyptian priest of On.

The healing art attained considerable maturity at a

very early age. Facts were observed and classified, and
deductions drawn, remedies were multiplied, experiments
made, and temples dedicated to Æsculapius. Knowledge
was accumulated and transmitted, and much that is useful
in medicine was known before the days of Hippocrates
or Galen.

In the fine arts no modern nation has ever been equal
to Egypt. Music, painting, and sculpture were cultivated among the Egyptians with a success to which no
subsequent age has ever yet *approached*. Greece received light from Egypt, and traced her footsteps. In
government, war, philosophy, poetry, and refinement, she
has never been surpassed. Do you ask for her law-
givers? History points to her Solon and Lycurgus. For
her orators? She pronounces the name of Demosthenes.
For her warriors? She mentions Leonidas and Xenophon. For her philosophers? She directs to Pythagoras
and Socrates. For her arts? She points to the Coliseum
and Parthenon, still rearing their summits in the sun-
beams. For her poets? She names Homer, and proudly
challenges the present or the past to mention his equal.

The human mind, though amply developed both in
Egypt and Greece, did not take the same direction in
both. Egypt cultivated the perceptive, Greece the reflective faculties. Egypt surpassed in arts, Greece in
science. Egypt observed facts, Greece drew deductions.
The former studied external nature, the latter the internal microcosm. The one cultivated the arts that adorn,
the other those that ennoble mankind. Egypt threw her
wand upon the pencil and the chisel, and bade the mar-
ble breathe, and made the canvas speak. Greece threw
her charm upon the heart, and hushed the passions into
calm, or whirled them into storm. The one *imitated* nature, the other *vanquished* her. The former arrested the
current of life in silent admiration, by her combinations

of color, form, and sound; the other held the heart pulseless by her vivid delineations of intense conception.

Rome followed Greece, but stopped far short of her. The impulse which the human mind had received appeared to have been in some degree spent before it reached the imperial city. Nevertheless, the works of ancient Rome are among the noblest triumphs of man, and her language is the repository of some of the richest treasures of human thought. Long as literature and science are cultivated, or the earth is the abode of man, the works of Tribonian, Virgil, Cicero, and cotemporaneous writers, will be subjects of the highest admiration. We need no other proof of Roman greatness than Roman language. It is precisely adapted to convey strong thought and intense feeling. We may form a very good idea of a nation's intellect by its language. That of France is just such as a versatile, volatile people, like themselves, would desire—formed for colloquial purposes. That of modern Italy seems designed for love songs, the only effort for which the emaciated mind of its inhabitants appears to be adapted. The language of old Rome is fitted for the most majestic movements of mind.

Under the influence of luxury and vice, Rome gradually declined, till at length she was overrun by successive hordes of barbarians, by whom the most valuable productions of her art were despoiled, and her land, which was as the garden of Eden, became converted into a desolate wilderness.

It is melancholy to behold the empress of the world, who had crushed beneath her iron footsteps Carthage, Pontus, and Judea, and whose chains, at one time, every nation, from Gaul to India, were proud to wear, trampled beneath the brutal tread of Huns, Goths, and Vandals. The reason was apparent. She neglected the education of her sons. It was not because she had no gunpowder

that she fell. She would have fallen with an armory in
every village, and a magazine in every house. Had she
possessed the spirit of her Cæsars, or her Catos, she
would have buckled on her shield, and her legions would
have rolled back the tide of invasion, and planted the
Roman eagle on the invader's soil.

This brings us to the third period, comprehending
those times to which posterity has assigned the appellation of dark ages. During the long period of nearly
ten centuries, the human mind appeared to have lost
nearly all its power; and the trophies which it had
before won were buried in oblivion. Universal darkness prevailed.

The monks were the only individuals who paid attention to literature and science; nor did *they all* devote
themselves to these pursuits—it was only here and there
that a monk became learned. The mass of civilized
mind was stereotyped, and appeared incapable of giving any other impression than that which the "Holy
Mother" delineated. The priests spent their time in
attending to the ceremonies of the Church, and the
Pope and cardinals were engrossed in managing affairs
of state. The whole earth appeared to be wrapped in a
pall of death, and the human race to proceed in one
great funeral procession of age after age to eternity.
The prevalence of Popery accounts for the condition
of the public mind during the dark ages. The grand
principle on which the Church of Rome stands, is that
the general intellect shall not be developed. Popery
and general education are as incompatible as light and
darkness.

The last period commences with the revival of letters,
and extends to the present time. The Reformation and
the revival of letters may be regarded as intimately connected, if not in the relation of cause and effect. It is

certain that no general revival of learning could have taken place without the influence of the Reformation. The grand question between the reformers and the Pope was this, Shall there be but *one* or *many* minds? There were many minor points, but this was the *grand* one. The Pope could easily have adjusted the numerous inferior matters in dispute between Luther and the Chair of St. Peter; but he could not yield his pretended right to control the world's intellect. He said, "There shall be but one mind on earth; namely, my own." Here Luther joined issue, and maintained that there should be as many minds as there are men.

Since the Reformation the progress and diffusion of knowledge have been both rapid and uninterrupted.

The discovery of the art of printing and the mariner's compass, the introduction of the Baconian philosophy, and the application of steam to the mechanic arts, have done much to prepare the way for general education. Several important political events have contributed largely to the same end. I refer to the American Revolution, the French Revolution, and the wars of Napoleon—the first resulting in the establishment of free government on our own shores, and the two latter in the breaking up of long-settled forms of tyranny and ecclesiastical usurpation, and all contributing to extend the belief that mankind ought to think for themselves.

We can but mourn when we contemplate the bloodshed of revolutionary France; but may we not conceive that even that disastrous event had a powerful influence in undermining the foundations of venerable superstition, extending liberal principles, and promoting general knowledge?

If we turn our attention to Europe, we shall find that a day of general knowledge has already begun. The parochial schools of Scotland have long been admirable.

The subject of general education receives much atten
tion in England; and although ecclesiastical and political
institutions present an insuperable barrier to the establishment of any efficient system of common schools ade-
quate to the wants of the British nation, yet legislative
and private munificence are sufficient to secure the blessings of education to the humblest walks of life.

The common school system is acquiring daily efficiency
and extension in France.   The Citizen King is acquiring
enduring popularity by elevating the general mind of the
great nation which he rules, and which has so often been
fertile in wars and wickedness.   There is much to com-
mend in the spirit which has long prevailed on the subject of the diffusion of knowledge in Switzerland, and
much to admire in the public and private institutions of
that independent people.   In Sweden the most liberal
views have long been entertained in relation to educa
tion.   She has a common school, supported at the public
expense, in every considerable town.   The University of
Upsal has an enviable reputation; and the general edu
cation is a prominent object of consideration with the
Swedish government.   The parochial schools of Den-
mark are equal to those of Scotland; and her metropolis,
Copenhagen, is one of the great centers whence radiate
the rays of science and civilization over the world.
Even Catholic Spain and Italy are awake on the subject
of education.   In Russia and Austria common schools and
seminaries are erected, teachers are educated, and an
ample course of instruction is pointed out by law.   Moreover, the children are not only provided for, but com-
pelled to avail themselves of the legal provisions for their
advantage.

Of the system of Prussia we need scarcely speak.   It
is the best that was ever devised, and will long be the
model for all the enlightened nations of earth.   Nearly

all the German states have imitated the Prussian system, and several of them have brought it to the same perfection as Prussia herself. If we cast our eyes toward Turkey and Egypt, we shall see that even the Sublime Porte has caught the general spirit, and transferred it to the Pacha, to spread over the land of Sesostris and the Pharaohs.

In our own country education is becoming general. To New England belongs the honor of first providing, by law, for popular education. Her noble example has been followed with various degrees of spirit and of wisdom by most of the other states of the Union.

The General Government has not been an idle spectator of these movements of the sisters of the confederacy. She has assigned to the new states—beside occasional donations—the thirty-sixth part of all the lands within their chartered limits for the purposes of general education. Indeed, to our country we must look for the origin of all those plans of general education which have been brought to such perfection in Europe. We believe that when the wisest of modern monarchs, Frederick William III, ascended the throne of Prussia, New England had a common school system matured by many successive years of reflection and experience. He saw America free; he believed her institutions would prove permanent; he knew that freedom was contagious, and that the example of America would be followed by the other nations of the world unless monarchies were rendered popular. To accomplish this object he devised an admirable expedient, namely, the education of his people, thus making the crown the source of the highest blessings that can descend from human governments, and endearing the monarch to his subjects. Many crowned heads have already perceived his wisdom and imitated his example. The throne of an enlightened people is a dangerous seat, yet such is the only kind of people that Europe will soon contain; and the question among monarchs is, whether thrones shall be abolished or made obedient to the popular will.

It is enough to make America blush to observe what despotic governments have accomplished with a system borrowed from ourselves. If republics, standing alone, can not endure without popular education, how can they stand in the light of monarchies which outstrip them in virtue and intelligence?

Although education is rapidly extending, much remains to be done before its universal diffusion. Millions are in total ignorance. It was the opinion of a late monarch, that out of ten millions of the adult population of a civilized nation, scarce one thousand were well informed. If we limit our view to our own country, we shall find much to be done. In some of the states the systems are partial, and in others radically defective. The necessity of universal education is obvious to all. There are *peculiar* reasons why education should be general in our *own country*. We need intelligence to bring out the treasures of our land—a land which, extending from the lakes to the gulf, and from ocean to ocean, and embracing almost every variety of soil and climate, offers unnumbered valleys and mountains to the hand of culture—exhaustless mines and numerous plants and animals to the scrutiny of science, and inestimable resources to the industry of freemen. We require education to discharge our duties as American citizens. All the machinery of government is moved by the hand of the people. The duties of juror, of soldier, and of statesman fall upon the ordinary citizen; nay, the highest functions in the cabinet, the forum, and the field *must* be performed by the common citizen, because Columbia knows no other.

Penn, in his preface to the "Frame of Government," remarks, "that which *makes* a good constitution must keep it; namely, wisdom and virtue—qualities which, because they descend not with worldly inheritance, must be carefully propagated by a virtuous education." There is a doctrine which teaches that general tranquillity can only be obtained by general ignorance, and that therefore education should be confined to the few, while the many are consigned to degradation and gloom. If there is any one that asks a reply to this argument, let him go to the history of the past, to the dark regions of barbarism, or the bright pages of revelation, to the indignant hearts of freemen pulsating around him, to reason, or to that voice within him which, though *still* and *small*, nevertheless speaks as the voice of God.

Education should be what its name imports. It is derived from two words—*e* and *duco*, which signify to lead out; and it means development. There is a very great error prevalent on this subject. Were we to consult the general opinion of parents, tutors, and pupils, we should suppose that education is the very reverse of development. When a parent directs his teacher in the education of his children, he informs him that he wishes them to have so much knowledge communicated, say of grammar, arithmetic, Latin, etc. He sends his child to *school* as he does to the merchant, to get so much, as though *knowledge*, like *cloth*, could be measured by yardsticks. The schoolmaster generally provides himself with a stock of the salable branches of education, and prepares to supply all orders in his line. He regards his scholars as the druggist does his phials. He takes their minds one by one, and pours in, pours in, from his larger vessel, of the required material, as though it were oil, and carefully corks it up, fearing lest the least motion should spill the precious article. The parent upon receiving his child acts upon the same principle, and examines the child's head to see if it be *full*. The poor child, too, always thinks of education as of a process of filling up. He goes into the school-room as he would go into prison, expecting to have his mind confined, and handled, and filled up, and shaken down. Now the truth is, that education is *following out* nature, instead of confining and crossing her. It consists in leading *out* the mind. The school-room should be an enchanted spot, and the child should enter it as the candidate for the prize entered into the Olympic games, or as the Indian engages in the gigantic pastimes of the wilderness. It is the arena for mental sport and mental struggle, with a view to mental development. An ancient teacher, Leucippus, understood the principle, when he directed the pictures of joy and gladness to be hung around his school room. I am aware that much useful knowledge is communicated in the halls of science. There is no branch of science which does not contribute its share of valuable facts. The *ordinary* branches of *English education* derive their chief value from being available to the practical purposes of life; but in reference to most branches of knowledge the primary object is the development, discipline, and strength of the intellectual powers. This principle will enable us to determine the question so much agitated in our own day in relation to the necessity of the classics and mathematics. I know that the demand of the age is for practical knowledge. We are becoming exclusively utilitarian. We cultivate a contempt for every thing which has not a practical application. The writings of several eminent men in this country and in Europe have contributed largely to give this direction to public sentiment. The general inquiry among parents is, what will enable my son to make money? Under the influence of a Carthaginian avarice the process of reasoning seems to be getting out of vogue. There is scarce any promiscuous assembly that can listen, for an hour, to a connected chain of thought. The only mental operations for which our age seems to be fitted, are arithmetical calculations and the memory of facts. It is not surprising that the classics and mathematics are sinking into neglect.

There are reasons why they should be studied independent of their power to train the mind. The latter are indispensable to the investigation of important problems in the natural sciences; and the former are serviceable by explaining the general principles of grammar, enabling the student to drink the waters of the purest fountains of classic literature, uncorrupted by translation, and giving him clearness and copiousness of language; but the great advantage consists in the exercise of abstraction, attention, and memory. If we overlook all minor advantages, and regard the classics and mathematics as instruments of mental training merely, and if we insist that practical benefits alone should be regarded in the education of the young, *yet* may we show that they are important. When the physician bids his dyspeptic patient to go to some distant spring, whose waters are *falsely* supposed to be medicated, does he act unwisely? What though the invalid obtains no medicine by his journey, may he not be benefited? The change of habits, of air, of scenery, of thought, of diet, and the healthful exercise of body, may co-operate to produce a cure of his loathsome malady, and confer upon him the highest blessings; namely, a *cheerful mind*, and a sound and vigorous body. Is it affirmed that a man derives no valuable fact from the study of the classics and mathematics? For the sake of argument we grant it; but then we declare that he derives blessings incomparably superior to a world of facts; namely, a strong, active, and vigorous mind.

2

In the ablest argument to which I ever listened against these branches of study, the principal reliance was placed upon the alleged fact, that students generally forget their classical and mathematical acquisitions soon after they leave the halls of science. I know that men rarely think of Euclid or Virgil when they are engaged in the ordinary avocations of life, unless they are engaged in professions which require an application of them. But what of that? Has the youth derived no benefit from his books and diagrams? Shall the man who has safely crossed the ocean dry shod, affirm, when he has landed, and has no more need of transportation over the waves, that ships are of no consequence? The chief advantage of books consists in their bearing the soul across the gulf which separates ignorance from knowledge.

It is impossible for an individual, however negligent he may be in relation to his collegiate studies, to deprive himself of their advantages. When a man has climbed the ladder whose foot is on the ground, and whose summit is in the sky, though every round beneath him should crumble into dust, he remains in his lofty elevation. Learning raises a man into the region of imagination, taste, and reason; and though her paths may be forgotten, her votary remains the enraptured spectator of a world of loveliness.

Besides the instruction to which we have referred, the natural sciences should receive a large share of attention, particularly philosophy, chemistry, botany, physiology, geology. These sciences are of especial importance to western Americans.

The *modern* languages are too much neglected in our literary institutions of every grade. They are worthy to be studied for various reasons, but chiefly because they contain much valuable information in every department

ot science. It must be a source of the highest satisfac-
tion to the physician to read the works of Bichat, Ma-
gendie, or Duchadela, in his own tongue, or to the divine
to peruse the works of the renowned Genevese pastor or
the amiable and elegant Fenelon, undiluted by translation.

It appears to me that special attention should be given
to the arts of speaking and writing. In this land, where
every man is liable to be called to take an active part in
the political discussions which agitate the country, and
even to represent freemen in the halls of legislation, it is
highly important that the student be early taught to
deliver his sentiments fluently and with effect. When
this art shall be more generally taught, the counsels of
wisdom will be less often overwhelmed by the declama-
tions of imbecility. Writing is no less important than
speaking. How often has the venerable minister, whose
heart was holy and whose mind was rich, perished from
the earth without leaving any thing by which the world
might be improved after his decease! I have known the
physician, whose fame extended from sea to sea, ridiculed
and pitied, because his composition was so slovenly and
ungrammatical that it scarcely conveyed the thoughts he
wished to communicate. Some of the ablest practition-
ers that ever attended the bedside of the sick have lived
and died in the western country. Had a Hines or Go-
forth written the results of his enlarged experience and
valuable reflections, the record would have blessed the
world long after the tracing hand "had forgotten its
cunning." The situation of our western fathers in their
youth precluded the acquisition of the necessary prelimi-
nary education, and hence their valuable knowledge was
limited to a small circle within the generation in which
they lived, and their names will be forgotten in the generation which shall succeed. *They* may be excused—

peace to their ashes!—but if their sons do not bless the world with the pen, on *them* and on *their* teachers must rest an onerous responsibility.

I will not detail all the sciences which ought to enter into a course of instruction; but before I leave the subject I will drop a remark in relation to the study of political philosophy. Our own Constitution should be studied in all colleges, seminaries, aɽd comn on schools. By the study of our Constitution I do ɪot mean the bare reading or committing of its articles, but the comprehending of them by tracing them to their origin through their development in the history of our country, and in the legislation of the government. I am happy to say that we have text-books prepared to our hand on this subject, and adapted to every class of scholars. The extensive dissemination among the youth of our country of sound and ample views of this great instrument would do more to save our institutions from destruction than any thing that can be devised.

It is not, however, by a knowledge of books merely that a mind can be properly educated. The mere book-worm is a useless animal, and, for aught that he does, might as well have never lived. He who would have a mind properly trained, must acquire a knowledge of men and things. He must learn wisdom from books and vales, mountains and cataracts. The earth and seas must be questioned, and the sun, moon, and stars made to yield their share of instruction. The child should cultivate acquaintance with nature, and be taught to woo her as his mistress; and, that he may acquire the indispensable element of round-about common sense, should be allowed to have free collision with his fellows.

Moreover, the youth should be made to emerge from the little circle of self, and to feel that he is an inhabitant of a deep and beautiful universe, which it is alike his duty and his privilege to explore; and he should be brought *up*, *up* from the little domicile of his father, and made to realize that he is a member of the great family of God, and that it is his duty to prepare himself to bless the world and all the future generations of man-kind.

Education should be more than the development of the intellect. Man is a compound being, and every element of his complex structure requires to be evolved. It has been the fatal error of mankind, ever since the revival of letters, to regard the youth as a mere intel-lectual machine. The wants of the body have been over-looked. One of these four results have generally fol-lowed: Either the individual has become disgusted with the paths that lead to fame, and retired before his frame sank beneath his toil; or he has become diseased and his life has been imbittered with pain and anguish; or, third, he has descended to a premature grave; or, lastly, he has become an idiot. A truant, or a dunce, or one whose constitution is as brass, may live under college discipline; but woe to the respectful genius who submits to college commons and collegiate restraints.

Go read the history of Genius. It is a history of in-firmities which no eye can trace without being moistened with tears. Is it reasonable to destroy our usefulness in cultivating our minds? Is it right to disregard the laws which God has written legibly in the liver and the lungs? As well blot out the decalogue as treat with contempt the handwriting of God on the visible temple in which his image dwells. Moreover, if man be disposed to run the hazard of meeting the frowns of God for the violation of his physical laws, and be willing to perish a martyr to fame, is it the surest way to attain the enviable summit for which ambition pants?

How often do we see the man of giant powers and

sanctified feelings, cultivated in the highest degree, sinking into the grave before he has been enabled to turn his noble powers to good account by the performance of a single important action! There is scarce a cemetery that does not read unheeded lessons to mankind on the folly of such a course. Many a name that is found only on the humble headstone of a new-mown grave might have been transmitted to posterity embalmed in undecaying glory, had its possessor regarded the fiat of Jehovah inscribed in the constitution of his earthly tabernacle.

Again: from a neglect of the body there often results a worse consequence than death itself. The mind is influenced by the body. This was known to the ancients, and passed into a proverb—*mens sana in corpore sano.* It was known before Rome was founded by one who said that much study is a weariness of the flesh. I have seen the mighty intellect gradually weakened by unremitting toil, till second childishness and mere oblivion succeeded Ulyssian wisdom and Homeric sublimity, long ere the golden bowl was broken or the silver cord was loosed.

It is not enough to develop the intellect and the body. There are other faculties besides the merely corporeal and mental. The moral faculties, above all others, are in need of training. The physical organs are the servants of the intellectual powers, but both are subjected to the moral and higher faculties. In consequence of the fall the latter have lost much of their power, while the mere animal propensities have acquired preternatural momentum. Hence, the highest object of education is to develop the conscience and the affections—those elements of man's nature by which he bears the image of his Creator, and which, if properly cultivated, will qualify him for a participation in the happiness of heaven.

It is astonishing that in this day of reform it should

be thought a strange doctrine, that education should embrace the culture of the heart. Long since was the question settled. It has been so regarded by the greatest lights in every age, from the last to that of Aristotle Locke, the most distinguished of modern metaphysicians, says: "I place virtue as the first and most necessary of these endowments which belong to a man," etc. Lord Kames says, "It appears unaccountable that our teachers generally have directed their instructions to the head with so little attention to the heart." "The end of learning," according to the immortal Milton, "is to repair the ruin of our first parents, by regaining to know God aright, and out of that knowledge to love him, to imitate him, to be like him, as we may be the nearest by possessing ourselves of true virtue, which, united to the heavenly grace of faith, makes up the highest perfection."

Many other illustrious authorities of modern times might be cited, but I pass to cite one or two ancient authorities Xenophon tells us with approbation that the Persians, rather than make their children learned, taught them to be virtuous, and instead of filling their heads with fine speculations, taught them honesty, and sincerity, and resolution, and endeavored to make them wise and valiant, just and temperate. Lycurgus, in the Constitution of the Lacædemonian Commonwealth, took less care about the learning than the *lives* and *manners* of the children. Aristotle surveyed man thoroughly. He was a great mind, perhaps the greatest the world has ever produced. It delights us to think of him. It makes us feel that we belong to a noble race, and that man can hold up his head, even when introduced into the presence of supernal beings. The name of Aristotle will be pronounced with reverence long as the noblest associations of genius, virtue, and morality can reach the human heart. Philip of Macedon, upon the birth of Alexander, wrote to Aristotle, saying that he thanked the gods not so much that they had given him a son as that they had given him at a time when Aristotle might be his instructor. Such was the veneration in which he was held by the greatest minds of his age. He ruled the empire of mind with undisputed sway for nearly fourteen centuries, and even now the chief acquisitions of the Spanish scholar consist of the logic and philosophy of Aristotle. This giant mind lifted the vail which hides eternity from mortal vision, and beheld, though dimly, its realities—he saw an immortal nature in man, and sought to frame his education so as to suit it.

Who does not feel that there is within him more than thought and sensation? Who does not permit his mind to go forth to the world to come, and inquire within him, how shall I travel up through the unwasting ages before me?

The world will soon be educated. It has been said that a similar progress may be traced in the general mind to what we observe in the individual. The world was once an infant, tossed upon the nurse's arms—it was hushed with a lullaby, "pleased with a rattle, tickled with a straw," and next she sallied forth to gather flowers on the lawn, and gambol over the mead, and next she could be seen creeping like a snail unwillingly to school; but now the nations of the earth give signs that the human mind has passed the periods of infancy and juvenescence; that upon it are coming the marks of sobriety and maturity, the spirit of inquiry, of thought, of action. The croaker cries that the world is degenerating. Is it pride, or ambition, or vanity, or ignorance which induces me to say that he knows not whereof he affirms; that the world, take it altogether, has more of majesty in her form, of grace in her mien, of vigor in her footsteps, of fire in her eye, of passion in her heart, of energy in her mind, than she ever had before? True, her old garments may cling to her, but she has outgrown them; and if she wear them it is because of her poverty. Her old nurse may compel her to rattle her childish playthings, but when she does so she feels ashamed—she is no longer charmed with the empty sound.

A spirit has gone forth among the nations which demands universal education. It comes upon the earth like the atmosphere we breathe, enveloping land and sea. It binds like the principle that wheels the planets in their orbits. Tyrants tremble, thrones bow, armies stand still before it. Man will be educated. On this point the extremities of the world meet—antipodes feel in unison—one hemisphere speaks and the other answers. Man may rise against it—avarice may utter its maledictions—superstition may rail—selfishness may exclaim, interested nobility condemn; but it comes. The decree has gone forth that man shall be enlightened. It will not be revoked. It is the voice of nature—it is the voice of God. Vain is resistance—vain the arm of law—vain the scepter of sovereignty—vain the barriers of caste. They will be swept like the dike before the tide when a nation is ingulfed, or the rampart before the whirlwind that has uprooted the forest.

If man is to be educated he is to be free. Freedom has always kept pace with the progress of education. Egypt was once free, at least so far as she was educated. She had, even then, many slaves, and so many untutored sons. Greece was once free; and why? Was it because her soil was fertile, and her valleys and her streams lovely, or because the fresh breezes of the Ægean or Ionian seas fanned her? No! Her scenes are as charming now as they were then. Greece was once free, but it was when the powers of her body and mind were cultivated—

when imagination, memory, taste, and feeling—all that
was bright or beautiful, foul or terrific, and magnificent
or lovely in wondrous, heaven-born, exiled man, enjoyed
an ample development and a vigorous life. Fix your eye
upon that colossal power issuing from the east, threaten-
ing to tame the spirit of Greece and reduce her to slavery,
by inflicting upon her sons a summary and awful ven-
geance for an insult offered to the scepter of Darius. It
reaches to the heavens, and casts a shadow upon a hemisphere. It rocks the earth beneath its tread, and threat-
ens to crush a nation at every footfall. How can a few
free cities in Greece resist? Will they not tamely sub-
mit without a struggle? Nay. The husband collects his
family around him, bids his little ones prove worthy of
their father after he shall have died for his country,
directs his wife, after the battle, to marry a man who
shall not dishonor her first husband, and marches to meet
the foe. The mother calls her son from the field, and,
suppressing her emotions, sternly says, "Take this shield
and go forth to battle. Bring it back, or be brought
back upon it." Now turn your eye to the pass of Thermopylæ. See that little band of three hundred Spartans
resisting, for three successive days, the Persian host of
five millions; and when at last, attacked *rear* and *front*,
they proceed to glorious death, see how they cut down
the ranks of the enemy as reapers in harvest mow the
golden grain!

Now direct your attention to Salamis—mark the im
mense fleet of Xerxes blocking up a few Grecian vessels
in that beautiful bay, determined to crush them at a
blow. One thousand Persian vessels float upon the waves.
and cast a bright reflection upon the waters from their
glittering prows. Mark those few Grecian ships sailing
gracefully down the bay; see! they station themselves
prow to prow against the barbarians—they commence the

battle—they plunge into the sides of the veering foe; they seize, they board, they grapple with the enemy body to body. And now the fight is over—the armament of Xerxes is routed and scattered—the maritime power of Persia is broken, and Greece is free. Why this indomitable spirit—this deathless love of freedom? Greece was then educated. That was the period when the song of her bard was as the song of the nightingale—when the voice of her orator was as the voice of thunder, and the whole mind of the nation breathed an atmosphere of freshness and fragrance.

Rome was once free—once mistress of the world From Gaul and Britain to Asia's remotest plains, she pushed her conquering march, and chained the subjugated nations, but she herself was free. Why? Her mind was developed and active. Wisdom sat in her councils, eloquence lingered on her lips. Her legislation was for the race—her literature for all time. Her poetry fell upon the soul soft and sweet as kisses from the lips of love. Her oratory vibrated upon the breeze as the notes of the harp, swept by an angel's hand.

Trace the history of modern Europe, and you will perceive that rational liberty has generally kept pace with the progress of general education.

Look at your own free country—the admiration of all lands, the glory of the earth.

Who were those, that, fleeing from persecution in the old world, sought an asylum in the wilderness of the new? They were the reading, thinking Puritans, who, on their landing, laid the broad foundations of colleges, academies, and schools. Who first rose against British oppression on our own shores? Who first raised the standard of liberty? whose swords first leaped from their scabbards for its defense? whose hearts first poured forth their blood around the soil in which it was planted?

Plains of Concord and Lexington, tell us! Hights of
Bunker, speak! Who first kindled the spirit of the Revolution all over the land, and kept the flames of public
indignation burning till the Revolution was consumma-
ted? The people who had been reared in temples of science, and who devised and put into execution the first
system of general education the world ever saw.

The angel of Liberty presses close upon the heels of
the angel of Light—and no sooner does the latter blow
his trumpet than the blast of the former breaks upon the
breeze. The education of the world will as surely be
accompanied by its freedom as daylight accompanies the
sun. Let a man know and feel what are his rights and
capacities, and he is no longer to be a slave. He will
govern himself. A still small voice speaks to every
bosom in the rational creation, bidding it be free—telling
it to enjoy the rights which Heaven has conferred, and
to acknowledge no distinctions but such as God has
ordained.

I do not say that monarchical governments are unnecessary when the public mind is ignorant. I think the
world's history shows that efforts to place freedom in
advance of intelligence have proved utter failures. When
a nation is untutored, a visible and imposing embodiment
of law, before which the multitude can tremble and bow,
may be a useful auxiliary to government; a Church Establishment may be proper to raise up advocates of truth;
a nobility may be requisite to secure an intelligent legislature; a standing army may be necessary for the national
defense: but once let a people be educated, and they are
themselves competent to all these purposes. The child
needs not the toy when the season of manhood arrives;
the youth escaped from his minority will dispense with
the services of his guardian.

It is said that in proportion as a nation becomes enlightened her distrust in her government will diminish—that she will perceive the beneficial tendencies of governmental regulations—that the monarch will become wise with his people, and will correct abuses and study public prosperity and peace—that crowns, and scepters, and nobles may be made instruments of blessing to community. To all this there is one answer: The wise man will not commit to another hand rights which he can as well exercise himself; or trust to another a duty which he can as well perform without extraneous aid.

The spread of knowledge will but extend evil if it be not accompanied with religion. Knowledge is power. It is so to the saint and so to the sinner; it is to the devil what it is to the angel. In itself it is neither good nor evil—a blessing nor a curse; but like the sword, it derives its character from the direction which its possessor gives it. A sword in the hands of a demon, infernal or incarnate, would be an unmitigated curse; in the hands of an angel of light, it would be an undeviating blessing. The one would employ it to destroy, the other to save.

Increase the power of any rational being before he is able wisely to employ it, and you increase his sin, and, by consequence, his misery. He is active; he will employ whatever of capacity he possesses. The more his capacity to do, if he do evil, the more his transgression; the greater his sin, the greater his misery. A poor German declared he would not educate his family, because as soon as his eldest son learned to write he counterfeited his father's name. He was resolved that if his children were inclined to do evil, their ability should be limited—they should be rascals upon a small scale. Experiments upon an extensive field in some of the nations of Europe have demonstrated that crime, instead of diminishing, actually increases with the extension of education, unless that education be accompanied with religious training.

This is precisely what might be expected. The evils which deluge the world are not to be traced to the intellect—their fountains are in the bosom. "A greater than Solomon has said," from within, out of the heart, proceed "evil thoughts, adulteries, fornications, thefts, false witness, blasphemies." This is the philosophy of truth— the philosophy to which every hour of the world's experience adds confirmation—the philosophy of God.

The heart is the seat of the moving powers. It is to the man what the pilot is to the vessel—it gives him his direction; the intellectual powers are the mere machinery. How vain is the hope of the world's perfection by means of its education! Let knowledge diffuse its rays to the ends of the earth—will sensuality, and avarice, and ambition, and jealousy, and vanity, and pride, and unbelief be destroyed, or even reduced? Nay, they will live and act; and act, too, in a broader field, with a keener eye, with a deeper wisdom, with a more refined art, and work out with more terrific enginery their desolating effects. Am I summoned to the ancient sages for proofs that education has a controlling influence over the passions? To ancient sages let us go. I am willing to search their caves, and groves, and public ways, and private walks, as with a lighted candle. I know that the closer the examination the more multiplied the evidences that my opinion is well founded. They taught what they did not practice. Their wisdom served but to refine their depravity and conceal its workings. The fountains of iniquity were calmer but more profound— the streams flowed in *narrower* but *deeper* channels.

There is one apparent exception—the son of Sophroniscus. There is no difficulty, however, in accounting for his superiority in goodness as well as wisdom, by considering that the true light enlighteneth every man that cometh into the world. A ray from the eternal throne fell upon his eyeball—he pursued it—and shall we deny that it led him to that Fountain where sin is washed away?

Am I referred to modern examples of distinguished greatness unaccompanied with religious feeling? I attend to the reference, prefacing, however, that we must be careful to distinguish between the effects of other influences and those of purely intellectual education. Lord Bacon will furnish us with an example of splendid endowments, united with varied learning. What was the influence of his peerless intellect upon his corrupt heart? Only to make its workings more refined and more destructive. Lord Byron is an example of surpassing greatness in an another department of intellectual exertion. And what effect did his education have upon his character and happiness? The poet has expressed it. He "was a weary, worn, and wretched thing—a scorched, and desolate, and blasted soul—a gloomy wilderness of dying thought." It is admitted that literature has a tendency to refine the taste, to open purer fountains of enjoyment than the senses, to exert a favorable influence upon the habits, to humanize and soften the character. But let not these tendencies be trusted too far; it may be doubted whether it is not the surrounding influence of Christianity, and not the intellectual habits of the educated, or the rank they hold in society, that lifts them above the brutal criminalities of the lower classes. It is the philosophy of the Bible, that each situation in life has its peculiar temptations. "Give me neither poverty nor riches, lest I grow poor and steal, and take the name of my God in vain; or lest I grow rich, and deny thee, and say, who is the Lord." Theft and blasphemy are the crimes of poverty, and pride and infidelity those of riches. Who shall say that the heart of Byron or of Bacon is less abhorrent in the eyes of

God, or less destructive in its influences upon man, than that of the poor sensualist, whose excesses are within the narrow circle of a few feet? The latter destroys himself; the former works the eternal undoing of millions besides himself.

You may educate your soul without religion, but you will only refine your misery. You may polish your speech without grace, but you will only sweeten the food of the undying worm. You may render brilliant the flames that burn within your bosom, but it will be only to add brilliancy to the conflagrations of earth and hell. Am I challenged to a comparison of educated and uneducated states? I accept the challenge. Admitting, for argument's sake, that some cities of antiquity, where refinement was found, were free from grosser vices, it may be asked, was not their superiority in moral character owing to their religion? For though paganism is false, it has a substratum of truth, and its influences in restraining the multitude are potent. But we challenge Athens, or Corinth, or Rome, in her attenuated refinement, to escape from the charge of criminality, as brutal as disgraced the darkest barbarism that ever found a place on earth.

Does more recent history present greater difficulties to our hypothesis? No; we rest the question on an appeal to the vices of the higher walks of life, and to the history of revolutionary France. Let the world tremble when she reflects, that education will enact the scenes of such a revolution all over the earth, unless religion accompany it.

Look around you. The world is arming; nations inert for ages are arousing their latent energies, bursting their bonds, enlisting under gallant leaders, and preparing for a struggle such as has never before been witnessed on the globe. She is calling the powers of nature to her aid. That army must either enter into the service of the prince of darkness, or enlist under the banner of the King of kings.

The Church must determine the world's course. She may, by purifying the fountains of instruction, give a righteous direction to enlightened intellect; or by neglecting them, leave infidelity to poison them all, and lead out perverted powers to the shock of battle with the Lord of hosts.

3

Mental Symmetry.

GREAT is the diversity among human minds; so great that it can not be fully accounted for by education, association, example—any thing, except original differences of mental constitution. These differences are owing, not to the introduction of new elements, but to new combinations; such combinations, too, are as endless as those of articulate sounds in human language. You will rarely meet with a man in whom there is not a tendency to excessive, or defective, or perverted action in some faculty or class of faculties. When an uncultivated mind is neither of great strength nor marked peculiarities, the ordinary intercourse of society and the common duties of life may be sufficient checks to its wanderings; but when a great genius is permitted to educate himself he usually becomes a moral monster. Such a one may have great learning, merit, success, but is rarely capable of just views, of safe and sober judgment. We might show the evils of ill-balanced mind, by tracing its influences either upon our usefulness, our happiness, or our salvation. That I be not tedious, I must limit myself to one of these three. Since the last is the most important, I select that. Let us trace the connection between mental and religious faith.

I. The want of mental balance is most frequently seen in the following faculties; namely, faith, attention, abstraction, and imagination.

1. Belief is one of the original powers of **the mind,**

and, like all others, may be conferred in various degrees; *generally*, however, it is strong in early life, so much so that we rarely find a child not disposed to indiscriminate faith. Not till frequently deceived do men learn to doubt. As their minds mature, however, they find it necessary to examine the grounds of their opinions, and this process is *then* a duty; but when they commence it while the intellect is still immature, especially if under the bias of depravity, without the light of experience, and under the influence of infidel or sensual associates, they are very likely to form a *habit of doubting*, which finally ends in contempt of sacred things, if not universal skepticism. Young men should be on their guard against this habit, and especially in these republics, where a feeling of independence is considered so becoming in youth. Very few, perhaps, are aware to how great an extent the power of belief is under the control of habit; they may learn something of it from analogy. What capability is not strengthened by use, and weakened by disuse? That power which can make the conscience either as sensitive as the apple of the eye, or as senseless as the cinder, can paralyze or galvanize the faculty of faith.

2. This faculty may be impaired also by an *exclusive* attention to the exact sciences, which accomplishes the sad result in various ways. It narrows the field of mental vision. How feeble the eye of him who spends life in a dark room, striking at minute points, compared with that of the sailor, accustomed to survey the broad ocean from the mast-head! so powerless is that mental eye which is trained to accurate discriminations and nice definition, in comparison with one which takes comprehensive views. The *great* mathematician, when he takes wide surveys of life and character, much more when he approaches that subject which fills both immensity and eternity, may be a

little reasoner. The immortal author of Celestial Mechan ism—La Place—is an impressive illustration. Illustri ous beyond comparison as a *professor of mathematics*, he was perfectly contemptible as a *statesman*. In less than six weeks, by his mistakes, as Minister of the Home Department, under the consulship, he forfeited his place. In the language of Napoleon, "His mind was occupied with subtilities, his notions were all problematic, his views were never right, and he carried the spirit of the *infinitely little* into the administration." No wonder that he had not sufficient breadth of view to scan the Chris tian evidences. Moreover, mathematical studies weaken faith by familiarizing the mind to indubitable evidence. This inclines us to be dissatisfied with every thing less. Demonstration proceeds by regular steps, inseparably con nected, accurately delineated, and leading to conclusions the contradictories of which are absurd. Moral reason ing advances through devious ways, by steps irregular, independent, and expressed only in ambiguous forms, to propositions the opposites of which imply no absurdity; hence, he who has long and steadily looked only at ab stract ideas and their relations, will be unable to appre ciate moral proof, however strong, as he who should spend years gazing upon the glowing fires of Stromboli would have an eye insensible to the soft charms of earth and skies.

3. Faith may be impaired by the habit of disputation. This is neither uncommon nor difficult to be acquired. That energetic exercise of the mind which is provoked by an antagonist is pleasurable, the applause awarded to superior information or intellectual prowess is very agree able, and the shout of victory is most refreshing to de praved human nature. Moreover, some men are prone to battle as the sparks fly upward. When such have weak muscles and strong minds they fight, like certain ani-

mals, head foremost, and, like the ram of prophetic vision, they often push their moral horns with equal facility
in opposite points of compass. Imagine a boy of good
parts and pugnacious spirit among inferior minds in the
district school. He overcomes in debate, one after another, all around him, till, flushed with success, and in-
toxicated with praise, he is carried by his comrades from
school-house to school-house, as a game-cock with gaffles
is conveyed to the neighboring roosts. At length he is
brought to college, and placed in a society which assigns
its members, without reference to their convictions, the
propositions they are to establish. It is easy to predict
the character of mind with which he will go forth into
the world. There are facts and arguments on *both* sides
of every moral question. Such a question can only be
determined by the mental balance. To use this properly
there must be patient observation, careful discrimination,
and a steady suspension of the scales; but for these
operations a mind under the influence of controversial
training is incompetent. The only two questions which
any subject admits of are, 1. What is the truth? 2. Is
this proposition true? The former is that of the philosopher—it leaves the mind free from improper bias, and
trains it to honest inference; the latter is the question
of the disputant—it stimulates the pride of the speaker,
and fits his mind to run athwart its most solemn convictions, in the eager search for middle terms. I will not
say that the office of the disputant is never useful, nor
that it may not be safely discharged when it succeeds a
process of investigation; but I do affirm that a controversial spirit, leading the mind, as occasion may require,
to undervalue *perfect* evidence and overrate *imperfect;* to
blend things of different species; to take advantage of
the ambiguities of language; to overlook facts important
to the issues, and bring in facts irrelevant; to confound

the incidental with the essential, the important with the trivial, the accidental with the uniform; to invert the order of sequences; or to rush rashly to general conclusions, has a tendency not only to mingle truth and error, but to unsettle, in the disputant's own mind, the very *foundation* of the power of belief. Talk as we may about the irresistible force of evidence, we all know that feeling warps the judgment, both directly moving the will to put the intellect in a wrong relation to the subject, and withhold or distort the proof which bears upon it, and indirectly, by influencing the train of association and giving tone to the mind. To have a perfect impression, we need both a perfect seal and a wax of proper consistence. If we at once mar the seal and harden the wax, what can we expect? The youth who leaves school a practiced debater will, in all probability, not only become a moral porcupine, the annoyance of every company into which he enters, but, by degrees, a thoroughpaced infidel He will be strongly tempted to assail the religion of his fathers, for the sake of always having an opportunity to gratify his propensity for combat and fondness for display; and, by repeatedly distorting the Christian evidences, and assuming a hostile attitude to the Gospel, he will finally become an *earnest* enemy of the faith.

The case of Chillingworth is an illustration. He would often walk in the college grove, and dispute with any scholar he met, on purpose to facilitate and make the way of wrangling common with him. While yet a youth, he produced, by his perpetual disputation on religious subjects, such a skeptical state of mind that he conceived it impossible to arrive at just views of religion. First he is vindicator of the Reformation, and the assailant of the Pope; presently he enters the Catholic Church, and becomes the defender of her faith; again

he returns to Oxford, and becomes the champion of Protestantism. He dwelt on the borders of absolute skepticism, if we may believe Lord Clarendon, who says Mr.
Chillingworth had spent all his younger days in disputation, and had arrived at so great a mastery that he was
inferior to no man in these skirmishes, but had, with his
notable perfection in these exercises, contracted such an
irresolution and habit of doubting, that, by degrees, he
grew confident of nothing. He was a great disputing
engine without an engineer. He had reason enough, as
Wood said, to convert the devil, yet not enough to convert himself. This spirit may exist in the Church;
foolish questions, and genealogies, and strivings about
the law, and doting about questions, and strifes about
words, whereof cometh envy, strife, railing, etc.—these
are indications of moral cholera.

But skepticism often results from a too great *facility*
of faith. There is a man who always holds the creed of
the preacher he last heard. Such were some of old
"driven about by every wind of doctrine; by the sleight
of men and cunning craftiness, whereby they lie in wait
to deceive." As you ride through the interior, perchance you see behind you a portly, well-dressed, elderly
gentleman, mounted on a bay steed, riding rapidly, as if
to overtake you. He is soon at your side, making your
acquaintance. You perceive by his portmanteau that he
is a country doctor, by his countenance that he is a sin-
cere, good-natured old man, and by his conversation that
he is a vain, garrulous, bookish, self-made, but not half-
made philosopher. He measures, with his quick, black
eye, your nose and chin, and describes your character according to Lavater; he surveys your cranium, and pronounces you a singer according to Gall. He inquires
your residence, parentage, and pursuit; but finding it
more blessed to *give* than to *receive* information, he tells

you the names and history of the settlers as you ride along,
and, when the village comes to view, he points out who
is its richest and who is its poorest inhabitant; who
keeps the best carriage and who the best piano. He
quotes Cicero, Aristotle, Darwin, Hume, Mohammed,
and St. Paul; he would that he was worth ten thousand dollars! and anon he is glad he is not, for he fears
the devil would set him at work. Presently he tells you
he does not believe there is any devil, and, finally, that
he devotes his leisure moments to fighting the devil and
the orthodox clergy. As he turns the corner of the
street, he presses you to call. Being delayed a day or
two in the village, you inquire into the doctor's history,
and learn that at eighteen he was a blacksmith, at twenty
a parson, at thirty a millwright, at forty a doctor, at fifty
a strolling lecturer on the quadruple subject of temper-
ance and geography, mnemonics and phrenology; that
he has, however, seldom had but one occupation at a
time, finding almost every year some new path to wealth.
In the year 1825 he could be seen, with radiant countenance, at the head of a company of merry youth, in the
valley of the Cuyahoga, planting yellow tobacco; in
1835 he was seen, with face beaming with joy, laying
off a city in some swamp near the banks of the Mau-
mee; in 1838 he is on the borders of Lake Erie, with
golden hopes, planting morus multicaulis and hatching
silk worms; in 1840 he is manufacturing beet-sugar in
the oak-openings of Michigan; in 1847 he is volunteer-
ing for the Mexican war; and in 1849 off for California. In religion he has tried all things, without, however, holding fast to any. In youth he is a Methodist
exhorter, thundering, flashing, denouncing, and pound-
ing the pulpit without mercy. Another decade of years,
and he stands, with long black robe, on the green banks
of some crystal Jordan, with head bathed in rich sun-

light, and knees trembling with emotion, while he addresses the multitude that have gathered upon the bridge, and the boys that hang like bunches of grapes from the surrounding trees. When a few gray hairs have found their way to his temple—a Presbyterian elder, he is leading his children up the aisle to be dedicated to the Father of mercies. The next half decade finds him, with broad-brimmed hat and drab coat, sitting in silent meeting, till the proffered hand gives token of departure. He soon becomes a Mormon, and then a Millerite; but, ere the decade is half out, he is a boisterous and defiant infidel, madly challenging, in the streets and in the papers, all and sundry, the parsons to debate with him.

Your curiosity prompts you to call upon him, and you find him in a long room, lined with drugs, books, and apparatus—books rare and ill-assorted; drugs botanical and mineral, in doses spoonful and infinitesimal; and apparatus to cure you either by wind-power, steam-power, or water-power. On his table lies the Koran, a copy of which he has just procured, and is now reading. He talks so as to give you no opportunity to reply; and to give you a proof of his boldness and skill, he assures you that the last time he was at Church he challenged the successor of the apostles to test his commission, by taking a dose of arsenic. You leave him with mingled pity and disgust, fearing that he is a *hopeless* case; but a year subsequent—inquiring after him—you learn that he was put into a state of clairvoyance and heard unutterable words, and since that has been a devoted Christian. Here is a man of several mental vices, the chief of which is a tendency to believe on insufficient evidence. Nor is he *raris avis*. In classic story we read of one whose body was so light that he was obliged to put lead in his shoes to prevent the wind from blowing him over—fit emblem he of many minds; and such minds, unless very favorably situated, are pretty sure to become skeptical.

II. The want of mental balance is found, in some cases, in the faculty of attention. Our ideas come in troops, and their character depends on fixed laws beyond our control. They gain admittance without asking consent, but depend for entertainment upon the will. Our power over them is twofold. We can place the mind in a region populated with good thoughts; we can dismiss intruders by neglect, and detain desired guests by civility. Attention is an effort to detain a perception in exclusion of others which solicit notice. This faculty is possessed by different persons in various degrees of strength, and in many is so weak as to be unable to direct the mind steadily to any object. Such a one passes life as in a pleasant dream. His mind is on the sofa to receive calls the year round; as the thoughts come and go it seeks neither information nor profit from them, and, its effort being entertainment, its recollections are like images drawn on the bosom of the wave. If all subjects are viewed carelessly, it is impossible that any but the most superficial should be understood. Conviction requires not only *proof*, but *perception*. The proof, even of religion, is not so obvious as to *force* itself upon a mind which gives it but a momentary notice. Though inattentive men may give revelation their *assent*, they have no basis of *conviction* to sustain them in the hour of temptation. Some men of this class blaspheme, others "care for none of these things;" others say they try to think, but can not. When they would meditate upon divine things, even on the day of rest in the holy place, or at the hour of stillness, in the retreat of secret prayer, other thoughts rush on them, and they find their minds like the fool's eyes Many of these persons, being pos-

sessed of some good mental powers, when they can be
brought to fix their attention, form correct judgments;
and, since common topics and temporal interests press
upon them constantly, they may be wise in little
matters and judicious in *worldly concerns*, while they are
fools in all that is *sublime*, and neglectful of *eternal* realities.

This class is numerous. Go into the streets and stores,
and you find multitudes who pay attention to things only
as they are *forced* upon them. Because politics, fashion,
and trade press themselves on the senses, and mix themselves with the passions, they are politicians, or dandies,
or tradesmen; and because religion does *not* obtrude itself on them, they know but little about it; they go to
meeting because custom or weariness leads them; they
hear of redemption, and grace, and regeneration, and
they suppose, because they have *heard* these terms so
often, that they *understand* them; but when asked to define, they find themselves in the situation of St. Austin
defining time, who said, "I understood all about it before I was asked, but now I know nothing of it." They,
perhaps, have no objection to religion, and can hear the
preacher without offense, or, may be, as one who has a
pleasant voice, and plays well on an instrument; but
since they are *unmindful* of his words they are *unmoved*
by them. They are infidels, as the modern Aristophanes
was. Mr. Boswell asked Dr. Johnson if Foote was an
infidel. "He is," said the Doctor, "as a *dog* is; he
never thinks on the subject." This species of infidel
may be found at all elevations of society, but particularly
at the higher, and especially in that portion of it which
has been raised suddenly. Of such it may often be said,
"Their houses are safe from fear, neither is the rod of
God upon them; they send forth their little ones like
a flock, and their children dance; they take the timbrel

and narp, and rejoice at the sound of the organ.   .   .
Therefore they say depart from us; for we desire not the
knowledge of thy ways.   What is the Almighty, that we
should serve him? or what profit should we have if we
pray unto him!"   Well may the Psalmist reason with
such: "Understand, ye brutish and ye fools, when will
ye be wise?   He that planted the ear, shall he not hear?
he that formed the eye, shall he not see? he that chas-
tiseth the heathen, shall not he correct? he that teacheth
man knowledge, shall not he know?"   We could forgive
the beast were he to receive his food without gratitude, and
regard his master without attention; but "the ox knoweth his master, and the ass his master's crib."   We
might pardon the brute should he murmur in the midst
of abundance; but, while "the wild ass brays not in the
midst of his grass, and the ox lows not over his fodder,"
the thoughtless sinner, forgetful of his almighty Bene-
factor, often utters blasphemies over his table.   We can
forgive the bird that sinks to roost at evening shade, and
rises up at morning light, regardless of every thing but
present pleasure and present pain—that gives no attention to its origin, interest, or destiny; but, alas! "the
stork knoweth his appointed time, and the turtle, and
the crane, and the swallow the time of their coming,"
while men, endued with reason, and moral sense, and an
apprehension of God, and a revelation of his will, can
spend a long life absorbed .in the petty interests of life,
and give no attention to any thing which does not gratify sense, or appetite, or animal passion.   .

III. Sometimes the want of mental balance is found
in the faculty, or process, if you please, of *abstraction*
By this we resolve a complex idea, and separately consider one or more of its elements.   This process can
scarce be overrated.   Without it neither the poet nor
the artist could form his beautiful creations.   His power

of combination were useless without materials. Whence can he obtain materials, but by abstracting from complex ideas? Without it we could have no philosophy; for what is philosophy but generalization? and this implies abstraction. Without it we could have no reasoning, at least of the demonstrative kind. Without it, indeed, what better were mankind than the brute? Deprive them of abstraction, and you rob them of language; deprive them of language, and you set them with the beasts of the field. Though all human minds possess it, yet some have it in so small a degree that they rarely attain to comprehensive views or general truths. They survey the fields that encompass their native village without ever reaching the ideas of vegetation or germination; they amuse themselves with the cat that purs at their feet, and the dog that bears them company, without thinking of the classes and orders of animated nature; they shiver in winter, and perspire in summer, without any notions of zones and latitudes; they whistle with their shopmates, and sing songs with their merry wives, without ever reaching the great idea of man; they look up to the heavens without seeing God. Whether they mark the moon walking in brightness, or the stars that glitter in her train; whether they hail the rising sun, or repose in the evening beams; whether they survey the well-poised central orb, or the planets wheeling in their spheres, they see naught but sights charming to sense— no goodness, nor order, nor might, nor design; these are all abstractions. Nor, hence, the glorious concrete which they imply—the great I AM. They walk the earth, or plow and plant it, or mold some of its productions into useful or beautiful forms, without perceiving the distinction between the instrument and the agent, the muscle and the mind. They think and feel, without thinking themselves up to the idea of soul; they seem lost in the visible, the tangible, the temporal. Of such the poet speaks in these words:

> "Fools never raise their thoughts so high:
> Like brutes they live, like brutes they die,
> Like brutes they flourish, till thy breath
> Blasts them in everlasting death."

What can such a one think of worship in spirit and in truth? Would you have him adore? You must give him something *visible*. Would you have him worship? You must put an *emblem* in his hands. How different the Christian philosopher! He garners truth—abstract truth—wherever he turns; he emerges from the limited circle of home and friends to survey humanity, and sympathize with its wants and sorrows; he distinguishes, not only between the vegetable and the animal, but the animal and the rational, the rational and the spiritual. By abstracting evidences of design from the face of nature, he obtains an impressive idea of an intelligent First Cause. By the same means he traces the wisdom, power, and goodness of the Creator; and, adding to them the idea of infinity and eternity suggested within him, he lives, and moves, and has his being in God. It was by a series of abstractions, for example, that Newton climbed to the top of the universe, and caught that glimpse of God which made him adore for the rest of life. By the same process he learned to see, like Moses, Him that is invisible through the smoke of Sinai, and, like Paul, Him that is eternal through the flesh of Jesus. Thus, too, an ancient, but not less worthy sage, who looked through the heavens to the glory, through the firmament to the hand, through the sun to Him that set his tabernacle; who, all through the spheres, heard a voice, and all through the earth saw a line; who, when he sought to cover himself with darkness, found the night turned to light about him, and, when he would hide within his own breast, found the candle of the Lord tracing his thought afar off. Do not misunderstand me. Men do not become Christians by *abstraction*, but by faith; but I would have you mark how abstraction and its attendant processes aid faith, and how the absence or imperfection of them may *predispose* to infidelity or *intrench* it. The best gifts may be perverted. There is a devilish abstraction often associated with great genius, which can go through all the works of God forgetful of his hand; can carry its lamp through all science without seeing him; can wing its way to all worlds, and sing its song under the gate of heaven, without thinking of him. Hellish metaphysics, that can abstract, for its contemplation, the earth—God's footstool—from his feet; the heaven—God's throne—from his majesty; the clouds—God's chariot—from his presence; the thunder — God's voice—from its teachings; the wings of the wind, on which he walketh, from the impress of his footsteps; that can even abstract the human soul from the universal spirit in which it breathes, and the universe from the arms which bear it up.

The Almighty has mercifully regarded human infirmities. In Paradise he walked visibly in the garden; in the patriarchal dispensation he conversed with men by his angels, and gave them altars and sacrifices for his worship. When he led his chosen people out of bondage, he put a cloud before them by day, and a pillar of fire by night. When he gave them a law, he did it in the midst of thunder, and lightning, and smoke, and an audible and mysterious voice. All this was adapted to a low state of intellectual cultivation, in which the mind was taken up with the outer world, having only reached the borders of the region of abstract thought. In the fullness of time, Christ came to preach peace, through his blood, in accents of mercy. Even under the present dispensation we are not entirely without aids for the mind in its ascent to spiritual things. We have churches, Sabbaths, ministers, and a few simple but significant symbols. He who *neglects* them is criminal; so he who *rests* in them. God is a spirit. The case of the heathen we are not called on to judge; but, surely, we, who harness the lightning for horses, may ascend the heavens to worship. The world is hastening to another dispensation, in which, perhaps, there need be no sanctuary built by hands; for no one shall say to another, "Know ye the Lord?" We are called on to prepare for this state of things, or for one analogous; for in the world where men are as the angels of God they need no candle, neither light of the sun, for the Lord God giveth them light.

IV. The want of mental balance is often found in the imagination—that faculty which, electing, with a nice perception, from the train of associated thought, the beautiful or the sublime, combines them, with a delicate appreciation of relations, in enchanting forms. This is the artist of the mind, and it decorates all her chambers with pictures and statuary, and perfumes them with precious odors. It may unbalance the mind either by its *excessive* or *defective* action. The former will carry it from the outer world to wander through Eden or through hell; the latter will make the real world one of mere blood and bones, of granite and grass. It is not my purpose to treat of imagination any further than it is related to the reasoning power; nor this, only so far as to show its influence on faith. For imagination is not only a soother of human sorrows, a builder of joyous homes, an enchantress leading the soul up the steeps of lofty conception to bright and boundless visions, but, in its sober moods, is the handmaid of reason, the friend of God : hence, skepticism generally denounces and affects to despise it.

Imagination aids faith by aiding its indispensable condition—apprehension. Every description is an outline merely, which imagination must fill up, to give it resemblance to reality, and make us feel the force of analogy in favor of its truth. It is needed in the interpretation of prophecy. The prophets speak in figurative language, and their words can not be properly appreciated by one whose imagination is torpid. It is requisite that we may feel the force of the evidences of revelation. The external evidences being adapted to the mass of mankind, in whom the imagination is generally strong, he who represses this power, to the same degree puts himself out of a proper relation to these evidences. The internal evidences are founded in the value of revelation; and since it is adapted to the *wants* of man, how can any one fully appreciate it who is unable to feel the great *heart* of humanity? and how shall one do this without the faculty which enables us to rejoice with them that rejoice, and weep with them that weep? The Bible points to scenes on high, and fancy helps faith to feel the powers of the world to come.

There is a large section of skeptical minds who, by an exclusive attention to natural science, extinguish all that is warming and expansive in the soul. These men would raise children as they do hogs, by placing them in favorable circumstances to fatten, and, when they are grown, would measure them with a three-foot rule, and weigh them in the hay-scales; would estimate their hearts by the pulsations at their wrists, and their brains by an electrometer. They would test the Bible by the rule of three, and estimate piety by the laws of physiology. They live in a world of exclusive matter, where all utilities are measured by inches, and all profit and loss denoted by dollars and cents. Surely, this is philosophy falsely so called.

Equally injurious is an excessive imagination. By

4

presenting every thing in distorted proportions, it pre
vents a correct apprehension of any thing; divorcing the
heart from the conduct, it unfits us for a right estimate
of morality; shunning the real world, it destroys our
sympathy with man, and our interests in what concerns
him—happy if it do not press us to the borders of derangement.   There are many skeptics of this class, of
whom Rousseau may be taken as a type.   Geneva, in the
early part of the last century, gave birth to this remark-
able man.   His mother dying young, and his father being engaged in the humble duties of an artisan, his
mind was permitted to grow as a vegetable in the wilderness, deriving nourishment from the soil in which
it was accidentally placed, and sending forth its branches
without direction or repression from human skill.   At
the age of seven he was an eager devourer of romances;
at eight he committed Plutarch's Lives to heart; at nine
he read Tacitus and Grotius; at ten he was placed in the
care of a country clergyman; and at fourteen he was ap-
prenticed to an engraver.   Running away from his master, he wandered upon the mountains of Savoy, till the
prospect of starvation induced him to renounce the
Protestant faith for the sake of a support from the
mother Church; placed in a monastery, he soon made
his escape, and, after many adventures, at length found
a patroness in Madame de Warens, of Annecy, with whom
he remained till he was twenty.   He then went to France
as music teacher, in which capacity he maintained himself with various fortune till 1742, when he was appointed
secretary to the French embassador of Venice; quarrel-
ing with his employer, he returned to France to resume
his former occupation, and devote attention to natural
science.   In 1750 he commenced author, and at different but not distant periods he composed numerous
works; the last of which excited so much opposition,

that he found it difficult to procure a resting-place for his feet, either in France or Switzerland. In a miserable and misanthropic old age, and after a fruitless, aimless, and romantic, though gloomy life, he found a grave in the Isle of Poplars. Though possessed of a mind of peerless power, a heart of exquisite tenderness, a style of surpassing beauty, an accurate knowledge of the human breast, and an extensive acquaintance with the world, his powers, because ill-balanced, were always questionably, often perniciously, employed.

His works evince knowledge that would honor Bacon, with ignorance that would disgrace a school-boy; principles worthy of Socrates, with sentiments that should shame a rake; imaginings gorgeous as Plato's, mingled with ravings like those of madness. But, to be more specific, the want of mental balance in Rousseau is evident both from his opinions and conduct.

1. His opinions are characterized by extravagance. His first essay, which drew the prize of the Academy, was written to prove that the re-establishment of the arts and sciences has been unfavorable to morality, which was evidently a hasty induction. In his essay on the inequalities among mankind, he maintains that savage life is superior to civilized—a notion which, being contrary to the sober judgment of the enlightened world, no well-informed, well-balanced head could adopt. In his Emelius, treating of education, he lays down, as his fundamental principle, that every thing should be left to nature—a principle which needs but to be stated to be refuted.

2. His works evince inconsistency. In the one last noticed he draws a lively and affecting picture of Jesus But in the same work in which he records this beautiful vindication of the blessed Jesus and his Gospel, he attempts to stab both to the heart, by representing Christ

us an impostor, and his Gospel as founded on false pretensions.

3. Absurdity. Though he courted flattery and relished favor, he was accustomed, late in life, to insult those who offered him the incense of their praise, and to interpret the world's approbation of him as a persecution instituted against him by literary men.

His conduct bears no less evident marks of ill-disciplined mind. It is characterized by extravagance. His demeanor in youth provoked his father to drive him from home; early in his apprenticeship he steals from his master, and runs away to avoid the consequences; next we hear of him as a footman, in which situation he repeats the crime of theft, adding to it that of perjury; escaping from service again, he is an outcast and a vagabond; soon we see him seeking shelter and food in a monastery, and anon breaking away to go through a series of adventures, till necessity brought him again to the door of the Church. But these are his years of boyhood. Let us trace his manhood. Dissatisfied with an occupation of his own choosing, he aspires to political favor; receiving it at the hands of Montague, he quarrels with his patron, and quits in disgust a post he had sought with avidity. Becoming an author, he attracts the popular praise by an opera, and then turns it into a storm of wrath by a letter on French music. By his work on education he draws from Parliament upon his favorite pages a condemnation to the flames, and upon his person a sentence of imprisonment; he provokes his native city, as he seeks an asylum within her walls, to close her gates against him, and send her hangman to burn his writings; he rouses the populace of Neufchatel, the city of his refuge, to compel him to flee at peril of his life; causes Berne to drive him from Peter's Island in the most inclement season of the year; and induces

England, who opened a peaceful bosom for his weary head, to look upon his retreating footsteps with the indignation due to a flying ingrate. Persecution, in itself, is no proof of a want of duly-regulated mind, but when it comes from all parties it is, *prima facie*. Rousseau was persecuted alike by Catholic France and Protestant Geneva; by fickle Paris and steady London; by pious bishops and infidel philosophers; by the unthinking crowd and the meditative Hume. We can understand how a man of good sense may, in this wicked world, in defense of some high and holy principle, provoke the opposition of all parties, but not how such a one can do so in endeavoring to *upset* all righteous principle.

Rousseau's conduct also is stamped with inconsistency. He writes a pastoral for the stage, and then inveighs bitterly against theatrical corruption. He praises integrity, yet changes his religion twice—once for bread, and once for protection. He writes a treatise on education, and commits his own children to the foundling hospital. While an infidel at heart, he professes the Christian religion. Advocating the purest morality, he is, by his own confession, a thief, a liar, and a debauchee. It was at an advanced age that he said, "I have been a rogue, and am still so for trifles which I had rather take than ask for." In reference to his licentiousness, his perfidy, and his want of natural affection, nothing need be said to those who know his history.

His conduct, in many particulars, is absurd. While with a stubborn infidelity he rejects the Christian religion, though his mind perceives its evidence, and his heart feels its purity, he receives with an easy faith the baseless systems of French philosophy, which teach that animal vigor is the perfection of man, and animal pleasure the acme of human happiness. He maintains the sufficiency of reason to discover a complete and comfortable scheme of natural religion, yet confesses himself agitated and distressed with his doubts. Professing love for men, he employs his matchless arts to infuse into their minds the poison which corrupts his own. Pretending to teach the science of happiness, he curses his own birth as a misfortune. Priding himself upon the inductive philosophy, he amuses himself with fanciful hypotheses. Strange compound of vice and virtue, ignorance and wisdom, prayer and blasphemy, faith and skepticism! It is easy to see in his mind the preponderating influence of imagination. Says Madame de Stael, "I believe that imagination was the strongest of his faculties, and that it had almost absorbed all the rest. He dreamed rather than existed; and the events of his life might be said more properly to have passed in his mind than without him—'a mode of being' which did not hinder him from observing, but rendered his observations erroneous. His imagination sometimes interposed between his reason and his affections, and destroyed their influence."

A few questions and inferences, and I have done. Have not those who have impaired their power of belief some excuse for skepticism? No more than the drunkard, who, by his intemperance, has disqualified himself for the practice of virtue. Are they not, however, deserving of peculiar sympathy? No more than the Christian, who professes Christ in prospect of the stake; the difficulty of belief in the one case is not greater than the difficulty of obedience in the other. Is not the case of such a one hopeless? Nay; because the will has power over belief. General Taylor, when asked the secret of his success at Buena Vista, said, "During all that bloody and unequal conflict, I never allowed myself for one moment *to doubt* that I should be victor;" and he expressed in these words a truth which every man feels. Moreover, the skeptic acts in common affairs on doubtful evidence. He can not demonstrate that he will succeed in business; that his money will pass; that his food will nourish him. If he has faith enough to preserve his natural life and secure his temporal welfare, he has enough to secure his spiritual life and provide for his eternal welfare.

If the want of proper mental balance disqualifies for correct judgment, does it not exonerate us from all blame for our errors? Nay; because the balancing of the mind is as much in our power as the subjugation of the affections, or the regulation of the life. I close with a few inferences:

1. Though a mind may be incapable of arriving at a correct judgment, it may, nevertheless, by reason of the charms of eloquence, or other advantages which it may possess, be the means of misleading others. Rousseau's essays upon the effect of the sciences, and the origin and progress of society, were among the fruitful seeds whence sprung the French Revolution of 1789—seeds which have reproduced themselves in the Revolutions of 1830 and 1848; mere logical sequences of that of 1789, and which are now leavening the whole mind of Europe, not with the principles of rational liberty, but with the various forms of socialism, radicalism, and red revolutionism.

2. The friend of man should aim not merely at the diffusion of knowledge, but at the proper training of mind. Schools, presses, books, lyceums, lectures are not enough. We must have institutions with courses of instruction so arranged as to produce well-proportioned and well-regulated intellect.

3. Nor is the regulation of the intellect all that is necessary. The sensibilities and the will must be developed and trained. The intellect itself is often well balanced.

How rarely does the world produce a well-developed man! Look into the Bible, and you may easily find a person distinguished in one or more particulars. A Peter, for example, gifted both in intellect and sensibilities, but deficient in will; a Solomon, mighty in intellect and will, but wanting in sensibilities. Rarely do you meet with a Moses or a Paul, equally able to reach a conclusion, feel an obligation, or execute a purpose. Look into profane history, and you meet the same difficulty. There are Aristotles who reason; Sapphos who can sing you almost into delirium with their utterances of intense emotion; and Alexanders who put forth will, till you tremble as in the presence of the Almighty; but not often do we meet with a Socrates, presenting, in fair and beautiful proportions, all the capacities and susceptibilities of exalted manhood. Nor have modern nations, with all their boasted advancements, been more fortunate than ancient. Here are the Bacons, with peerless reason; there the Napoleons, with matchless will; and there the Byrons, with morbid passions; but where are the Luthers—good, sound, symmetrical men?

4. The tendencies of the age seem to oppose the full development of humanity. Let me be understood. I refer not now to the proposed improvements in education, which have a direct tendency to make monsters instead of men; but to the progressive division of labor. It is separating society into castes as distinct as those of India. There is one class running into brain, another into tongue, another into eye, another into foot, and another into hand, so that it will soon take the whole human race to make one great human animal. The different classes are like so many wheels in some great complicated machine, each one worthless without the rest, and each individual, instead of being the world in epitome, is like a cog in a cog-wheel. I grant that this division of labor

secures wealth, art, and civilization; and if the great object of God in creating man was to beautify the world, I
would have no objection; but if not? God does not create man for the world, but the world for man.

The Inner World.

A Y, there is an inner world, and into it I would invite you. I would not depreciate the outer; it is worthy to be occupied—worthy to be studied, even by angels—worthy, though cursed, of its almighty Maker; its paths—so full of melody, and fragrance, and beauty—are fitted to lead to heaven, and the starry vault which overhangs them is a suitable portico to God's eternal temple. Praised be God for the world of matter, and all its accompaniments!—for the air, which not only fans the lungs and purifies the stream of life, but, at our bidding, wafts our most secret thoughts and feelings to our beloved fellow-minds; for the waters, which not only fertilize and refresh the earth, but bind its continents and islands into one brotherhood; for the light, whose vibrations enable us to touch the most distant planet, and whose rich beams overspread both earth and sky with charms!

> "My heart leaps up when I behold
> A rainbow in the sky;
> So was it when my life began,
> So is it now I am a man;
> So let it be when I grow old,
> Or let me die."　　　　WORDSWORTH.

Praised be God for the body of mysterious senses and capacities—worthy to be the servant of a rational soul during its earthly pilgrimage, and, after having been purified in the tomb, to become a partaker of her everlasting life!

But there is another world—a world which the "vul-ture's eye hath not seen and the lion's whelps have not trodden"—a world whence float all those thoughts that flow over the universe and make it a volume of truth—a world in which, scorning the present, we range at will the future or the past, and, heedless of place, we share infinity with God.

When shall we enter into it? Not prematurely: "tarry at Jericho till your beard be grown." Nature designs that the early years of life should be devoted chiefly to the development of the body; hence she entices her new-born man to the green bosom of the earth, and the warm embraces of the sun, and the full baptism of the fresh and fragrant air; hence, too, she fires him with irresisti-ble longings to see, to taste, to feel, to leap exulting in his new-made powers. Thus she nourishes, and cher-ishes, and molds him into man; thus she gives him

> "A spirit to her rocks akin,
> The eye of the hawk and the fire therein."

At the same time she fences up the borders of the inner world. Meanwhile the goodly land of thought is germ-inating; and about the time of its first ripe grapes, when the outer world loses some of its charms, let the inner open its gates. This opening, however, requires pa-tience, perseverance, retirement. Perceptions being more vivid than conceptions, we can not without effort attend to the latter in exclusion of the former. When we turn the mind's eye inward, we must either resign ourselves to the train of suggested thought from which we awake as from a dream, or we must fix our attention upon some one of the series, in which case we soon become weary, as one listening to the same frequently-repeated note. If we attempt to analyze our mental state we become per-plexed; for although in the outer world we are familiar with the succession of events, in the inner we find all at first in confusion. No wonder we usually remain in the wilderness of external things till some strong passion, or sense of duty, or accidental circumstance, impels us inward. Alas! how many pass through life without scarce feeling that there is a world within!

Vaucauson, the celebrated mechanician, had his taste for mechanics excited accidentally. In his boyhood he was frequently shut up in a room where there was nothing but a clock; to amuse himself he studied its construction, till, at length, he became acquainted with its parts and their relations and uses. Ever afterward he found his·delight in mechanics.

Happy for many a man would it be if he could be shut up where there was not even a clock, so that he might be forced to examine the wonderful machinery of the spiritual time-piece—the immortal soul—till he understood its parts, relations, and uses! How much more likely would he be to set it by the Sun of Righteousness, that its pendulum might swing in symphony with the spheres, and its hands go round the circle of duty in harmony with the heavens! Habitual inattention to the outer world greatly promotes attention to the inner. The more we live the life of sensation the less we do the life of reflection. "For the flesh lusteth against the spirit, and the spirit against the flesh, for they are contrary to each other." It is said of Democritus that he put out his eyes in order that he might study philosophy. The story is probably untrue; but it is certain that Poesy put out the eyes of Homer and of Milton before she lifted the vail from their glorious spirits. I pity you not, blind old bard of Scio's rocky isle, as you roll in vain your quenched eyeballs to find a ray of light, for so much the more melodious was the epic that you warbled through the listening cities of your native seas! Nor thee, thou second Homer, but greater than the first, do I pity, as you sweep from your well-tuned lyre those plaintive pentameters:

> "Thus with the year
> Seasons return; but not to me returns
> Day, or the sweet approach of even or morn,
> Or sight of vernal bloom or summer's rose,
> Or flocks, or herds, or human face divine;
> But cloud instead and ever-during dark
> Surrounds me."

No; I pity you not, because so much the more didst thou wander "where the Muses haunt"—so much the more did "celestial light shine inward," and raise up things invisible to mortal sight.

The patience, study, and retirement requisite that we may look inward will be well rewarded; for,

1. The inner world is a new one. The youth usually knows as little of it as of foreign land. He has, it is true, vague ideas of it, as he has of orange groves and palm-trees of which he has read but never seen. It were glorious to discover even an unknown island. Columbus, as he was approaching the New World, was accustomed to close each day, in the midst of his assembled sailors, on deck, with a solemn meditation and a hymn of praise to God. On the evening before he saw the land, and while he was gazing at the indications of its near presence, he sat musing at the stern, and as he inquired, "What is the world upon which I am entering? who are its inhabitants? how will they receive me? and what will be the consequences of my landing to myself, to Spain, to the world?" his feelings became overwhelming. But within your breast, immortal man, there is a still more glorious world. Columbus could take possession of America in the name of his sovereign only; he was to leave it almost as soon as he touched it; he could not give so much as his own name to its shores. The undiscovered continents of thought that lie within your breast you

may name, and hold, and occupy at will and forever.
That country which Columbus discovered was seen by
millions of eyes before he saw it, and has been by millions since; but the world within you is unlike all others,
and no eye but yours can behold its scenes or trace its
revolutions, except the all-seeing One.

2. This world is one of *beauty*.   Lovely as is the outer
world, it has no beauty in comparison with the exceeding
beauty of the inner.   The beauty of material things is
but one; that of the mind is threefold—the beauty of
the present, of the past, and of the future.   I know that
not *all* within is beautiful.   There are marks even in the
soul of dislocation and disorder; there are chasms, and
storms, and deserts, often more awful than those of the
external world; yet over the whole a grandeur, like to
that of archangel ruined, reigns.   The heavens and the
earth are drawn within us in those forms in which the
soul has most delight; the past, too, is there, according
to the affinities of our minds.   It is prevailing disposition that paints the panorama of remembered thought,
and cherished joys that display the figures of the foreground; and as the canvas of memory stretches, the
more charming scenes of the foreground acquire greater
relative prominence, so that remembrance gives us, with
ever-increasing vividness, the scenes of our earlier and
happier hours, when Nature presented itself with all the
freshness, and beauty, and purity of youth to our light
and loving hearts.   The village green of our boyish
gambols, and the oak which first shaded our heads, and
the bower where we first told our love, are the first objects on which the inner eye rests when it turns to the
past.   And then the persons—who are they?   Those
whom we first loved—and how? in their happiest moods
and their sweetest expression.   Do they now slumber in
the narrow house?   We see them not writhing in the

agonies of the death-bed, or cold and motionless in the
shroud.   Memory can say, "O, Death, where is thy sting!
O, Grave, where is thy victory!" for she gives us back
the dead even in the loveliest forms they wore.   The
poor, bereaved Irish emigrant, when he forgets the desolation of the present, and looks into the past, sees not
the darkness of the tomb.   Hark!

> "I am sitting on the stile, Mary,
> Where we sat side by side."

What does he see?   Hark!

> "And the springing corn, and the bright May morn,
> When first you were my bride."

Even though the specters of past sins and the shadows
of departed sorrows arise, they come before us with soft-
ened and solacing tints, and melt the soul into a salutary
tenderness, which is often felt to be luxurious.   The
future, too, is within.   Hope—the busy artist of the
mind—runs forward and paints the approaching scenes
in light; and though the picture perpetually vanishes or
darkens behind him, the mental limner never tires, but
rushes onward, ever busy and ever brightening the future
The beauties of nature are *fixed;* not so the beauties of
the mind—they are changeable at will.   As the genius
pores over his mental treasures,

> "Anon ten thousand shapes,
> Like specters trooping to the wizard's call,
> Flit swift before him.   From the womb of earth,
> From ocean's bed they come; the eternal heavens
> Disclose their splendors, and the dark abyss
> Pours out her births unknown.   With fixed gaze
> He marks the rising phantoms: now compares
> Their different forms, now blends them, now divides,
> Enlarges, and extenuates by turns,
> Opposes, ranges in fantastic bands,
> And infinitely varies."

The beauties of nature are attended with deformities.
The mind can present us with thornless roses and un-

mingled fragrance.   Milton's Eden blooms with beauties
that can be combined only in the soul.

The beauty of the inner world is an *independent* one.
It is only poetically that matter can be said to have
beauty at all; philosophically, beauty, like color and fra
grance, belongs exclusively to spirit—

> "Mind alone. Bear witness earth and heaven,
>   The living fountain in itself contains
>   Of beauteous and sublime! Here, hand in hand,
>   Sit paramount the graces. Here enthroned
>   Celestial Venus, with divinest airs,
>   Invites the soul to never-fading joys."

The outward world, I know, wakes up the beauty slum-
bering within; but, in return for the favor, the soul
throws its own charms over its senseless forms.   He who
would see a paradise without must first make a paradise
within; then as his soul passes out through the senses,
she will make ever new discoveries of beauty from the
reflected hues of her own fancy, and will give every hill
and promontory a new name, and derive from it a new
joy, from its resemblance to some picture which the inner
eye alone has seen.   Hyperides once pleaded for a guilty
woman; but finding that his eloquence was vain, he drew
the vail from the beautiful bosom of his client, and won
his cause.   O could I but expose the beauties of your
own breasts, I need not add,

3. That the inner world is a *sublime* one.   Great extent
is sublime.   Hence, in part, the sublimity of the sky,
the expanded seas.   He who is confined within the
boundaries of sense dwells in a narrow house; he who
abides within occupies a large space.   Deprived of all
his senses, he may walk abroad, and, even on his couch
of straw, enjoy a liberty that tyrants might envy, and a
range that sensualists can never know.   Is depth sublime?   Who has stood upon the verge of the precipice,
and looked from cliff to cliff? did not his eyes grow dim

and his brain reel? God has said, "The heart is deep."
Plummet line may fathom ocean; but who hath sounded
the depths of human passion, or human reason, or human
will? In thy breast is the whole history of man, past
and to come, in epitome; for in it are the fountains
whence all human actions flow. Look into the deep well
of thy heart, and thou shalt see down into the heart of
Adam. From the depths of thy reason thou canst draw
up the ladder that raised Newton to the skies. Untutored slave though you may be, within thee are all the
elementary principles of that philosopher's immortal dem-
onstrations. Although thou canst not take the dimen-
sions of the rice-field that limits thy labors, thou hast
within thy mind the mathematics that can measure and
weigh the most distant planet in space. Is swiftness
sublime? Ask the lightning. But thought mocks its
lazy foot. It touches all things with a celerity that is
nearly equivalent to ubiquity; for it oversteps a space
that, for its distance, can scarce be measured, in a time
that, for its shortness, can scarce be noted. Is mystery
sublime? How mysterious are the faculties of the mind!
Imagination is the image of omnipresence. It soars
backward, or upward, or downward, as on wings of light;
or rushing onward, with the mien and the majesty of an
angel, it may cross the boundaries of creation, and having perched on the limits of possibility, may spread its triumphant wing, and proudly perform its gyrations on the
clouds beyond. Memory is the image of omniscience.
It unrolls a canvas on which earth and skies are out-
spread; so that though the eye may be closed, the soul,
within its little tenement, can examine all the hues and
forms of sensible things in its impressions of the past.
It sends its telegraphic wires back to the green of our
earliest gambols, and, pushing its magnetic lines through
the tomb, it brings us messages from eternity—the thou-

sand joys, and kindnesses, and loves of the lost and
redeemed ones.   Reason is the image of divine wisdom.
It gives us a knowledge of relations—in proportion to
which our views expand.   With nothing but perception,
conception, and consciousness, we are fettered in mind
as one bound to a stake would be in body.   By tracing
relations, we break our chains, and extend our walks
farther and farther through the universe.   Reason often,
like the architect, looks along the chain of causes and
effects, and sees results of which the agents that are to
produce them have no conception.   How little progress
would men make without its speculations!   Say that
speculation is a shadow; yet by a shadow Thales learned
to measure a pyramid.   Say, with Aristophanes, that philosophy is in the clouds; if some one had not been there,
who would have calculated eclipses?   Say, if you will,
that the lines of scientific light are intangible and imaginary; so are the solstices and ecliptic; but the sun
observes them, and the heavens are taught by them, and
the year is divided by them, and commerce, and history,
and law, and love fall into order by their guidance.   Say,
if you will, that the speculative reason wheels in air;
and what shall we say of the earth which spins on nothing, yet bears you safely?   You rejoice in maps, and dial-
plates, and steam-engines, and railways, and telegraphs;
but all, all, were first drafted in the reasoning soul, as
the universe was drafted in the mind of God before it
uprose from chaos.   Even when the labors of enlightened
reason do not result in any material benefit, still they are
always improving, always desirable, always grand.   How
superhuman appears Pythagoras pointing out that system
of the universe which it required twenty centuries of
subsequent observation and study to demonstrate!   How
.grand Seneca, when in remote antiquity he predicts the
discovery of a new world upon our planet!   How angelic

Roger Bacon, projecting his mind so far forward of his age that his cotemporaries deemed him an infernal being, and subsequent times, whose discoveries he had anticipated, looked back upon him as a supernal one!

How grand a movement of mind is generalization! What a wonderful pregnancy does it give to words! Each general term is a swarming city of thoughts—a word may describe a weight which the planet Jupiter could not carry on his bosom, and a few figures, that we play with as a child with its toys, may be made to lift the screen from the immensities of Jehovah's works.

And what shall we say of the will? which says to the wilderness, bloom, and it is as the garden of Eden; which says to the mountain, be open, and the bowels of the rock are blasted out; which makes a path through the sea, and a pillar of cloud and fire, on an iron pathway, through the desert; which tameth the tiger, and maketh a plaything of the lion; which grasps the impending thunderbolt, and hides its powerless flash in the bosom of the earth? And O what awful power does the will sometimes exert within the dominions of the soul! See that martyr laid upon the rack! Every limb is stretched, and every nerve thrills with agony. A single word, and the prisoner will be relieved and restored to his friends. How shall he avoid uttering it? Will not his *intellect* rebel? Will not his *heart* cry out? Will not his *tongue*, for an instant, break loose? Wait and see. Hark! the heavy instrument falls, and a bone is broken, and the sharp fragments pierce through the quivering flesh. An interval follows—a dreadful interval—and, in the midst of the agony, the executioner demands the word of recantation; but that tongue, which utters forth groans that make a city shudder, lisps not a syllable. Slowly the instrument descends again, and another bone is broken, and another, till every limb is in fragments

and the whole body lies lacerated and bleeding; and now
the executioner approaches, and the dews of death are
upon the martyr's brow, and though the tongue speaks
sweetly and freely of Jesus, and of the land where the
weary rest, it is mute as the grave as to recantation.
Zeno, on the rack, lest his tongue should betray him, bit
it off, and spit it out in the face of his judge. The
human will is, perhaps, the most sublime of all things.
That Power which wields the lightning and moves the
storm, which scatters worlds through space as the husbandman casts seed into the furrow, which by a look
of terror could blast the universe, suffers the will of man
to rise up against itself. How terrible looks the fabled
Atreus, glutted with his banquet of revenge, when the
justice of the gods comes down upon the feast! Bolt
after bolt falls on every side, yet the untamed will of the
rebel, as if in triumph, looks up from the sea of fire, and
cries, "Thunder, ye powerless gods; I am avenged."
And such a scene—yea, and more dreadful—do we see
every day enacted in the sinner's breast, where the will
sits, amid the ruins of the soul, an outcast from God,
and, though on earth, like Satan in the pit, saying, in its
desolation, as it approaches the tomb,

> "Hail, horrors! hail,
> Infernal world! and thou, profoundest hell,
> Receive thy new possessor."

There is a power behind the will as awful as the will
itself—the heart. This is the image of creative energy.
To a great extent it shapes the character, molds the
words, and directs the actions of men. Give me a perfect knowledge of a man's heart, and I can give you his
character and course in general results. The judgment,
I know, is the informer of the heart, and the memory,
and the fancy, and the will, and the conscience, and the
providence of God, are its checks and modifiers; but

upon all of these, except the last, it has a reflex and most potent influence: sometimes blinding the judgment, giving tone to the fancy, forcing the will, and perverting the conscience. Hence, it is that part of our nature upon which chiefly the fires of depravity burn, and upon which, too, the dews of grace distill.

We are accustomed to give too much credit to intellect in the works of creative genius. Poetry, eloquence, etc., are the spontaneous results of influences little heeded and little understood. Genius, in its happiest moods, when throwing the hues of sensible things over the regions of the spirit, or the coloring of the soul over the scenery of the earth, is but sweetly yielding to the laws that shape the thoughts of the infant on his hobby. While the poet may think that he is steering his heart, his heart may be directing him, telling him where to stop in his spiritual journey, compelling him to survey the scenery around him, and even pointing him to the very colors in which he should dip his brush. The philosopher who is indignant at the prejudices of others may have his own intellect tinged with unperceived prejudices, expressed in the very words in which he declaims against the errors that he exposes. The revolt of the common mind at what seems artificial, and the great law of criticism which condemns every thing that does not seem natural, shows how little of the achievements of a genius are due to his volition. To give the mind such a tone that its spontaneous suggestions shall be worthy to be uttered—this is the labor of the heart.

The heart is the index to the faculty of association. Every hill, and river, and blossom which presents itself to us opens a department of thought, and lets loose a crowd of images, grand or mean, useful or pernicious, according to our previous trains of thought; and these trains of thought depend chiefly upon the heart. To the holy, for example, every scene brings the animating revelations of Scripture, and awakens the transporting hopes and exalting charities of the child of God; his mind always moves on consecrated ground, and his march is in a triumphal procession of sanctified saints to glory and to God; he communes with the white-robed and pure, and lives rather in the tranquil past or the jubilant future than in the dull and sinful present. For him roses are roses of Sharon, and lilies are fragrant with incense. For him Christ stands and teaches amid his apostolic band, or even in the desert; and angels leave their heavenly bowers to gather round his new-born soul in the hour of sorrow and of trial.

And who does not know the influence of the heart on the judgment? Why do poets sing better and oftener of a lost than a recovered Paradise? Why is it that genius planted in the soil of righteousness and the air of worship produces only a few fading leaves, while in the ashes of sin and the atmosphere of moral death it breaks out into gorgeous luxuriance? Why is it that the Hebrew melodies are sought after by the few, while the Don Juan is craved by millions? Why is it that the works of wickedness are often as impressive as the tempest, while the melting beams of holiness are unheeded as the sun? It is because of the power of the heart to warp the judgment.

The heart is the source of inventive genius. Will can not bring up a single thought; the heart is the wizard that evokes, shapes, and directs them all. I know it does not make thought any more than the mountains make the springs that gush from their grassy sides; but, like the volcano, it heaves up mountains within the mind, and makes a channel which gathers up and whirls the spiritual waters as they fall, and rolls them in deeper and deeper currents to the sea. It does more: it disturbs

the electricity of the mental clouds, and opens the sluices
of the inner skies. Let the heart be excited, and the
mind needs no schoolmaster in order to express itself.
What one man feels he can make another feel. I would
not despise criticism or rhetoric, but we had Homer and
Pericles before either. Love can pour music from its
throat without a gamut; can ascend the sky, like the
prophet, in its own chariot of fire; can thunder and
lighten like unto him that walketh upon the wings of
the wind. Don't undertake to instruct it. The eagle in
his eyrie needs no anatomy in order to fold his wings
around his triumphant heart, no physiology to direct his
course to the morning sun. The excited soul thinks of
no rules, and requires none; it seizes its figures and
arguments without a consciousness of its movements, and
hurls them with an energy that is like to supernatural.
Sometimes it seizes and drops, builds up and destroys,
engages and terrifies, with a confusion that abides no
criticism, and *heeds* none; for it is the confusion of inspiration—an inspiration to which, however wild, common sense and philosophy alike respond in the hour of
its triumphant action. Would you see one of the grand-
est images of God? See the heart of Milton brooding
over the chaos of his mind, and shaping and animating a
universe beneath its wings, and filling the hights, the
depths, the paradise, with upper, nether, or surrounding
fires. Would you bring out *fully* the power of the mind,
you must light up a consuming fire in the breast.

Now, in order that I be not thought transcendental,
consider that although thought flows on according to the
general laws of association—contrast, resemblance, conti-
guity, and cause and effect—these are modified by coex-
istent emotion, frequency of renewal, peculiarities of
mental constitution, etc., and that these chiefly depend
upon the heart; finally, that the stimulus imparted to

the mind by intense emotion both determines its affinities and gives the tendency to suggestion by analogy, in
which principally consists the charm of genius.

4. The inner world is sublime, because of its influences. These extend indefinitely, but immensely, both
through space and time: each moral world is related with
many others. You see that star high up in the skies;
should it leave its orbit, this earth would be shaken—all
worlds would feel its erratic movements. Look at your
soul. Its movements may be felt in hell, in heaven,
raising a new wail in one or a new song in the other.
The wandering of a planet affects only matter; the wandering of a soul affects rational and immortal mind. So
in *time* the soul is felt afar off; it may pass from earth,
yet still live beneath the sun: the oak dies, but the acorn
lives. Truth springs from truth as seed from seed;
though with this difference, that the crop, while of the
same nature as the seed, and much more abundant, is not
always its exact copy. The acorn will produce an oak to
the end of time; but the Illiad may produce an Æneid
in this age and a Paradise Lost in that; while it is bringing forth an epic in one mind, it may be producing an
ode in another, a tragedy in a third, and a philosophical
oration in a fourth. The history of Thucydides produced the orations of Demosthenes, and the novels of
Sir Walter Scott the historical works of Guizot and
Theirs.

Action is no less prolific than words. He who has no
children may, nevertheless, have a numerous and illustrious progeny. His character, like Newton's, or Wesley's,
or Washington's, may be a fruitful parent. Marathon
was the mother of Thermopylæ, Thermopylæ of Salamis,
Salamis of Platæa; the battle-fields of Greece begat
those of Rome, as Cannæ and Philippi did those of Gaul
and Britain; Bunker Hill and Yorktown have descended

lineally from the first mountains and fields of martial glory. The tomb of Leonidas, as long as an oration was annually delivered from its side, produced a yearly crop of heroes. The dead body of Lucretia, planted by the hand of Brutus, brought forth the living liberators of Rome; and the wounds of Cæsar's corpse, touching Plebeian sympathy, as Anthony lifted up his shroud, were the seeds whence sprung the tyrants of ten centuries. The blood of the martyrs was the seed of the Church. Hail, Archimedes! though the sphere and the cylinder have moldered long since from thy tomb, I see thee to-day. Hail, Demosthenes! though thy voice has long since died away over thy native shores, it heaves many a living breast about me. Hail from thy grave! Hail, Paul! though Nero long ago claimed thy head, thy heart beats sacred music in a thousand pulpits to-day.

5. The inner world is eternal. Those seas must dry up and these mountains dissolve, the sun itself shall burn out, and the lamps of this temple of night may drop from their sockets, like autumn's withered leaves, but the soul of that good man shall never die. It is the holy of holies which God's chosen ministers watch over, and which mortal eye may not see; and it shall be removed with reverential care, when the clothes of this tabernacle of the body are folded up, and its boards are taken down in the grave. The faculties of his soul are holy things, which go not into darkness, but shall have an entrance ministered to them by angels of light into the temple not made with hands, where they may abide with God forever.

Such a world, young man, is thy soul; and wilt thou be dependent on external things for thy happiness, so that thou art sad or cheerful according as the wind blows hither or thither? Rather be like him whose soul is his country—his own dear native land—and to whom neither cloudless skies, nor perennial spring, nor double harvests can yield so much delight.

When we drink the bitter waters of life, or loathe the surfeit and the pestilence of its pleasures, or burn with the sting of its fiery serpents, let us go home. O glorious truth! that the mind, shut out from this scene of sensible things, can retire into its own infinite domain, and, as it moves along, arrange all things into order and symmetry by an untaught yet unerring astronomy! Thrice happy he who finds that spiritual immensity a sanctuary, sprinkled with the blood of the Lamb, lighted up with the lamps of angels, radiant with the presence of God, and perfumed with his perpetual blessing. To such a one even the dungeon is the vestibule of heaven, and the scaffold a step in the ascent to glory. He can say,

> "Should fate command me to the farthest verge
> Of the green earth, to distant barbarous climes,
> Rivers unknown to song, where first the sun
> Gilds Indian mountains, or his setting beams
> Flame o'er Atlantic isles, 'tis naught to me,
> Since God is ever present, ever felt,
> In the void waste or in the city full."

How grand a sight is the launch of a ship! As she moves from the stocks slowly down the inclined plane, with a few shouting sailors upon her deck—as she booms for the first time into the bosom of the waters, and rises and proudly rights herself upon the waves, you think of the fate that awaits her, the rich cargoes she is to bear, the multitudes of living men that she is to hold up on her planks from the deep, billowy grave; of the communion she is to establish between distant continents; of the messages of love and the lessons of light that she is to bear to the nations; of the storms she may encounter, and the lightning that may smite her masts and wrap her sides in flame, lighting up the sea as if in mockery of the night; of the many that may plunge down from her burning bowels to rise no more, and the few that may float over the spray upon some half-burnt plank, and you feel a swelling at the heart. But what were this scene compared with one such as God might show you, if he were to convey you beyond the milky way, and point you to a new world which, perhaps, he is at this moment lanching into space! Could you see the wide landscape of mountain and lake, and light breaking forth, and creation becoming warm and living; fields turning into flowers, waters floating with birds, lands bringing forth cattle, the very dust, on some fragrant eminence, turning into two human but not immortal beings—their nostrils dilating and their bosoms swelling with the breath of God—the surrounding stars crowded with excited angels, and the new seas and skies becoming vocal with the song of the sons of the morning—how would you feel? Suppose you were informed that the conduct of that new-made pair was to determine the future character of that globe; whether, as its valleys fill up with population, it shall roll onward in deeper and deeper darkness or into higher and higher light; whether it shall float in cursing and groans, or in thanksgiving and the voice of melody—how would you watch and pray over them, as if the blood would rush from your eyes and the soul sob out of your body! But the lanch of a single immortal soul into life is a grander and more awful sight than the lanch of such a world. The happiness of those millions of successive generations would cease in the grave; their misery, however intense, would terminate in death. Take the most joyous conceivable life of one of its inhabitants, or the most intense agony of another, and multiply it by millions of millions, and you have still but a *limited* joy or sorrow; but that immortal soul carries wrapt up in itself a happiness or woe that shall know no limit. As it sails out in life, it is to determine whether it shall float in the blackness of darkness forever, or circle in eternal light around the throne of God.

Miscellaneous Reading.

THAT we may keep within proper limits, let us confine ourselves to two inquiries: How shall we read? and why? And, first, how? My answer is, with scrutiny, reflection, and appropriation.

I say with scrutiny. And this remark is not unnecessary, for often a book is used to dissipate weariness, fill up a vacant hour, or direct our attention from subjects which might lead us to laborious thought. That there are occasions when books may properly be used in this way I do not deny; but books suitable for *such* purposes hardly deserve that name: let them be ranked with toys—well enough for the child, the valetudinarian, the way-worn, and the poor, bewildered one who wanders on the brink of derangement. I speak now of *serious* reading, which ought always to be an exercise of thought. If you find your mind unengaged, lay your book down, lest you form a habit of mental supineness. If it is of great importance, take it up again, but not till you have called your soul to account for its listlessness. Many often read even the Bible merely to satisfy a tender conscience, or conform to a commendable habit, till at length it produces no more impression upon them than blank paper. If they were to pause, search, study, *pray*, over each verse, or if they were to read it in the original language, especially if they were under the necessity of tracing words to their roots, of declining nouns and conjugating verbs, it would be a new revelation to them.

To read with scrutiny implies attention—an active, fixed, penetrating state of mind, which should be directed to the words, the thoughts, the object, and the spirit of the author. We can not apprehend ideas without understanding words, for it is only by words that we can either think or receive thought, or convey it. Many who read words which they can not define, suppose they understand them, more especially if such words are familiar to them. They may, indeed, by a sort of instinct, and they may not. If they do, it is only by supplying conjecturally the words not defined. In matters of importance it behooves us to be *sure* that we are right. Most words have synonyms; but if they have been correctly used, they can not well be exchanged for others. Let us see that we give to each word not merely the right meaning, but the right *shade* of meaning. And here you will mark one of the great advantages of classical study; it directs attention closely to words; it qualifies us to trace their relations; it habituates us to scan their uses. You will not infer that we are to define all our words, but that we are to be *capable* of defining them. We must attend to *construction*, no less than words. The same words may be arranged so as to convey truth, or falsehood, or nothing at all, of which we have many examples in the responses of heathen oracles. How often do we read on carelessly! If we understand, very well; if not, just as well; if we get a meaning that satisfies us, what matter whether it is our own or the author's! How differently do lawyers read deeds and wills, replications and declarations, statutes and decisions; the dotting of an i or the tense of a verb may make all the difference between defeat and victory. They relate in classic story that a client returned to his lawyer a speech that he had written for him to read to the jury, saying that when he first read it he thought it perfect; when he read it the second time he began to doubt; and when he read it the third time he thought it miserably poor. "You fool," said the lawyer, "are you going to read it to the jury three times?" Most authors write for the world's *first* reading, and the world rarely gives them a second. In general, books are read superficially; if addressed to the imagination and the passions, because it is *useless* to fathom them; if addressed to the reason, because it is *difficult* to do so; if of irreligious character, because they fall in with the current of human thought and feeling; and if of opposite tendency, because they are unwelcome to the heart. How many sublime passages in the prophets, the Psalms, the evangelists, are of no meaning, because we do not make ourselves acquainted with their force! Let us give every book a third reading, or, at least, its equivalent, before a final passage. Hence, it would be well for us to have always upon the table an English dictionary, and a Biographical, a Geographical, and a Scientific one, that we may understand the allusions and feel the full power of the author. A good book read with constant references, whenever necessary, to maps, history, and authority, is worth a cart-load read superficially; it exercises our highest faculties, extends the circle of our information, and revives, deepens, and applies knowledge previously acquired. From the ideas of the author we must ascend to his design. Many have read Homer's Iliad, for example, without ever comprehending its purpose; yet it is not till we see the lesson it is designed to impress—the importance of fraternal union—that we can fully appreciate the great poet's power. How can we judge of a book without considering the intention with which each illustration, argument, deduction, and figure is introduced, and the relation it bears to the writer's ultimate purpose? A thing absolutely strong may be relatively weak, a thing absolutely impotent may be relatively mighty; a strong chain may be rendered useless by one missing link; a feeble beam may become powerful, if it leap out of the timber in answer to the stone that cries out of the wall. Nor should we fail to consider the *spirit* of the author—the habitual nature of his feelings, and their particular state when he penned his production. Thus the spirit of Shakspeare is genial; of Young, gloomy; of Milton, grave; of Byron, bitter and malignant. Yet no one of them has written all his works in the same mood. Compare, for example, the Don Juan and the Hebrew Melodies. Without appreciating the spirit of an author, we can neither understand the meaning, nor measure the intensity, nor fix the comprehension, which we should ascribe to his expressions. The same words are of far different meaning and force in the mouth of anger and the mouth of love; the same phrase in Solomon's Song, and in Moore's Melodies might inspire feelings as different as would an angel in light and a woman in scarlet. There is one book which, in consequence of its antiquity, its pre-eminent importance, and its inspiration, should be read with *special* aids; that is, commentaries. I refer now to such as are critical; of which Adam Clarke's is a fine example, though, like the sun, it has spots. There are separate commentaries on particular portions of Scripture which will generally be found better than any universal one. I wish we had writers who had done for other books of the Bible what Lowth has for Isaiah and Horne for the Psalms. The diffuse commentaries, abounding in reflections which had better come from your own mind, you will generally find watery; you may obtain ideas from them after long waiting, but they will not be your own, and they will be received in a distended and weakened mind. Educated men often read the Bible better without commentaries.

Let them have a good Bible dictionary and a work on Archæology; an acquaintance with the original tongues, and with ancient history and geography, and they need not fail to find the meaning of holy oracles. Moreover, they will study with a mind more awakened, more independent, more cautious, more critical, and more reveren-tial, too, as the principal and the auxiliary, the divine and the human, will not be so intimately blended. Were commentaries all destroyed, the Bible would become a California, where every man, assured there was gold, would wash his own sand.

To *scrutiny* should succeed *reflection*. We should not only examine superfices, but penetrate, revolve, evolve, separate, compare, combine, till "out of the eater comes forth meat, and out of the strong comes forth sweetness." We should seek not merely for the melody of the cadences and the beauty of the images, but the validity of the judgments, the weight of the matter, the value of the conclusions, the additional illustrations and arguments by which the statements and reasonings might be corroborated, the relation which the facts bear to our previous knowledge and the various uses to which the information imparted may be applied; or, on the other hand, the exceptions which have been omitted, the blunders which have been committed, the inconsistencies into which the author has fallen, and the inapplicability of his subject to useful purposes. A book read with reflection is like the imaginary gold concealed in the vineyard of fable, which, causing the possessors to dig deep all over their grounds, formed in them habits of eager industry, and gave to their soil an unsuspected productiveness. Men too often, either from a want of information or want of independence, from an overweening confidence in the author or an incorrigible indolence in themselves, from an unpardonable haste or an unfortunate weakness, re ceive all that they read. Such minds are like human life, never in one stay. Their philosophy is grass; in the morning it cometh up and flourisheth; in the evening it is cut down and withereth. If you would know their present state of mind, ask what book they have last read. "They are ever learning, but never able to come to a knowledge of the truth." Their minds are as blackboards overspread with symbols, which by cancellation yield only zero. If they happen to be pastors or teachers, woe to their flocks or pupils, for they are to be led through a maze; if they are doctors, woe to their patients, for they must taste a little of every thing. Happily such persons have but little force.

There is a great want of reflection among mankind; the multitude in all ages has sunk into the grave without thinking; and the few that have not, with here and there an exception, have been occupied with the thoughts of others rather than their own. A few sovereign minds divide among themselves the realm of reason, giving opinions as decrees. No sway more perfect than theirs. Talk not of Russian autocrats in presence of the autocrats of philosophy, who, as God's thinking vicegerents, prescribe routes and limits for the outgoings of human mind, and hunt down those who transgress them as wild beasts of the desert. Hence, notwithstanding unnumbered millions of separate immortal men have lived upon the earth, all the thoughts of the world that have been preserved may be ranked under a few heads: thus, Plato, Aristotle, Confucius, Mohammed, Bacon, Kant. A Cæsar or Bonaparte ceases to rule when he dies; but these mental despots rule ages after they disappear. Aristotle, for example, swayed Europe for more than a thousand years, and still he sways. Columbus will be remembered long as an island or mountain of this continent shall stand above the

waves; but Homer will be known long as a syllable of
language lives upon the lips of man. Columbus rules
not the lands he pointed out; Bacon does. It would
seem, at first sight, that the law of hereditary succession
does not prevail among the princes of thought; but,
upon examination, we see that young ones are but the
children of the old, with altered names. Scarce a new
phase in philosophy that is not a mere revival of an old
one. The present age is as unreflective as its prede-
cessor; it is one of activity and haste, in which its very
facilities are incumbrances; the multitude of its books
discourages reflection. Would you form an idea of a
man's politics, ask what political paper he takes; would
you know his religion, ask what preacher he hears. But
do not his opinions direct the choice both of paper and
preacher? So you might suppose, but that you find
him veering as they do, just as they veer when their
masters do. What revolutions are wrought in the masses
by the movement of some national convention! "Old
things pass away, all things become new;" parties are
bought and sold with their leaders, as Russian serfs are
bought and sold with the land. Men will not think;
they have their thinking done for them—done by machinery. As the Carguero carries the traveler in a chair
on his back over the mountains of Quito, so the teacher
is to bear the student on his blackboard to the summits
of knowledge; as the priest in Siberia ties his devotions
to the windmill, and expects every revolution to count a
valid prayer, so we expect our ministers to waft our souls
to the mount of God; as the steam-horse puffs us,
whether we are asleep or awake, to the city, so we expect
the book to bear us to the metropolis of reason. Hence,
human mind, with increased activity, has diminished fer-
tility; amid advancement in arts, and sciences, and
wealth, it is stationary in the higher grounds of intellect-

ual labor; having more leisure, more facilities, more knowledge, more incentives than it has ever had, it is content to be agitated and amused with the successive explosions of the magazine of folly and error, and makes no majestic march in the direction of truth. It trembles to ascend on the stream of borrowed thought to original fountains, as if, like the rivers of Eden, they were guarded by sworded cherubim; it fears to move onward to the ocean, as if beyond the frequented coasts of truth nature inverted her laws. Reflect as you read, cautiously, but freely, boldly.

We should not only read with reflection, but *appropriation.* The mind may comprehend its knowledge, and act upon it, without being able to make use of it; hence, some, though very learned, are far from wise. Their minds are as a storehouse, where all treasures are confusedly mixed; they are walking libraries, and can give you history, philosophy, poetry, and theology, but just as they received it; they have carefully wrapped their talent in a napkin, and buried it, to be disinterred when called for. There are others, who analyze propositions—who consider the relations of facts to others which they have previously acquired, and thus elicit further knowledge, uniting the different colored rays of the mental prism to form a perfect light—who ponder principles till they see new applications of them—who examine arguments till they perceive new truths which they may be made to disclose—who find in one sophism the clew to another. They profitably invest their talents, and give forth knowledge not as they received it, but, though like itself, yet not itself, *more* than itself; the spiritual corn, sinking into their mental soil, dies, and is quickened, and sends forth first the blade, then the ear, then the ripe corn in the ear. Between the knowledge of these two there is the difference of life and death. It is amazing what power of appropriation a man may acquire. Kossuth may make a speech every day from the conversations of men, who little suspect that the knowledge they receive from him is but that which they have given, though bearing the impress of his mind; he received it as ore, he returns it as currency. See that your soul is not a great cistern, but a great furnace, in which every thing cast must be saved as by fire.

Not every book is to be read with the same degree of attention. Erasmus cries, "I have spent twelve years in the study of Cicero." Lord Verulam responds, "O ass!" Generally that book which has been written hastily should be read hastily. Some volumes have cost twenty years' toil; these should be read slowly, or not at all. Although we may tithe mint, anise, and cummin, we should not be as long collecting the revenue of a poor district as of a rich one. "Some books," says Lord Bacon, "are to be tasted, others to be swallowed, and some few to be chewed and digested." Of the last class I speak.

The habit of attentive, reflective, appropriative reading may not be easily acquired, nor is any other good habit; but we may say of it what Aristotle says of learning, "The *roots* are bitter, but the *fruits* are sweet." When once it is acquired, it may readily be strengthened, and will afford through life a never-failing feast and an unceasing mental growth. Youth is the time to acquire it, and the best mode is to use the pen; not to transcribe important chapters or beautiful passages to be used as aids in argumentation or gems in composition—a practice which enervates memory and degrades style; nor to construct commonplaces—an exercise much more useful; but to form discourse of your own; this will prove a magnet to gather fragments as you advance, and at once guide and stimulate your further excavations.

But read with an eye to human life. We should not **live** to read, but read to live. Action is the highest mode of being—

> " In the deed —the unequivocal, authentic deed--
> We find sound argument."

The purpose of training a child is not so much that he may read, or write, or speak, but *go*. Mere study is a weariness to the flesh; and however diligent we may be, wo can not grow much wiser or stronger by reading exclusively. Books need the illustration of nature and life. The physician, lawyer, doctor, warrior, who should spend life in the study, would not be fit to be trusted. It is only by the *application* of knowledge that we learn its limitations, exceptions, and proper force. Hoarded knowledge, like the hoarded manna of the desert, putrefies; and epicurism in mind, as in body, has its acids and crudities, its flatulencies and constipations. All wisdom and wit that does not promote man's happiness or God's glory is vanity. Hence, while men have ranked philosophers and orators as demigods, they have ranked discoverers and inventors as gods; and properly, since the comet that occasionally flashes up the heavens is less godlike than the dew which, from day to day, and generation to generation, invisibly distills upon the earth.

Neither a nation nor an individual is to be judged by the number of its books. Egypt was crumbling when her Alexandrian Library was the largest in the world; Asia Minor was falling under the blows of Greece when her books were ten to one more than her adversary's; Greece had multiplied her parchments when Rome's hardy legions subdued the Peloponnesus; Rome was filled with books when Alaric sacked the imperial city. On the contrary, Greece had but few writings when she drove back Xerxes, and produced Homeric song; Rome few when she expelled the Tarquins, and brought forth

Brutus; Britain few when she drafted the Magna Charta, and sent the Black Prince to Cressy; and what is more common than to find a man with a large library a very great fool!

Nevertheless, books have their uses; and we come to inquire, secondly, why should we read? The lighter uses of reading—to tranquilize our passions, to assuage our sorrows, to moderate our anxieties, to beguile our journeys, to give interest to our idle hours, to refine the manners and humanize the heart, to awaken the desire for knowledge and form the taste for reading—we pass with a single caveat against a class of books which is usually employed to answer these indications: I mean novels and romances. In condemning them let us not be understood as denouncing *all* fictitious productions; the fables of Æsop, the allegories of prophecy, the parables of Christ, the tales which embellish and impress historical facts, and the illustrations which the pulpit employs with so much grace and efficiency, afford at once authority for fictions and rules for its construction and use. Novels and romances usually offend a pure taste and a sound mind by their gaudy dress, their unnatural characters, and their paucity of instruction; and always tend to weaken the power of attention, to impair the judgment, to divorce the connection between action and sympathy, to give a preponderance to the imagination, to create a distaste for simple truth, and a disinclination both for manly studies and the dull realities of life. Many of them are liable to a greater objection, as, by a Plutonic chemistry, they turn the diamond of virtue into the charcoal of vice. It is alleged that they soften the heart and excite an interest in suffering. Often, however, it is an undistinguishing or a mawkish sensibility, which, while it can weep over the picture of a dead Gipsy, can wring the living heart of a loving father. That by inflaming the imagination, interesting the affections, and exciting an interest in books, they may be useful to some minds, and, indeed, to most minds in certain moods, must be admitted; but since the good they accomplish may be effected by works of unquestionable tendency, why resort to such as intoxicate while they imparadise, bewilder while they allure, and emasculate while they excite? The higher forms of poetry, philosophy, and religion are sufficiently fascinating and energizing to all the faculties.

Let us come to the higher ends of reading—to inform, to balance, and to stimulate the mind, to form the style and to reform the heart.

To inform the mind. The great purpose of education is to develop and train the faculties; in doing this we must necessarily give some information; but the college, when she graduates, turns you over to testimony or observation. It was the error of the schoolmen to suppose that all knowledge was contained in the soul; hence, they wasted life in seeking to find out external things by agitating their own intellects, as if matter could be made by shaking emptiness. Although the theory of the schoolmen has been exploded, their practice has not. We still need to be reminded that we can not draw conclusions without premises; that from nothing comes nothing, however much it may be agitated. In judging, remembering, analyzing, and generalizing, the philosopher may have great advantages over the savage; but for the *facts* the one is as dependent as the other. An educated young man has fundamental knowledge of nature and life, of history and geography; but let him remember that his knowledge is but fundamental—that he must build upon it, and that his very foundations are liable to decay unless he is constantly carrying forward the superstructure. History, civil, ecclesiastical, and natural, are before him. Of the first two he has an outline—general

notions of the stream of time; names of nations, **their
rise, decline, and fall**; great epochas, leading events, distinguished names, and a table of dates—a mere chart to
give interest and direction to the voyage before him   So,
too, of natural history—his knowledge is but skeleton, to
be clothed and animated by a patient continuance in the
study of nature under the guidance of its more eminent
interrogators.   In this department of learning, if we be
not studious we must ever recede.   Chemistry, geology,
etc., have just passed the pillars of Hercules, and are
cutting with their keels an unknown ocean toward an unknown world.   Geography, once a fixed, is now a progressive study, following commerce, and science, and Christian sympathy into all regions, and mapping past events,
human progress, and providential designs among all peoples.   But what shall we read upon these subjects?   I
give no list of books; but, since by reading according to
a well-conceived plan we shall have clearer views and
speedier progress, I refer you to some such "Hand-Book
of Literature" as Bishop Potter's.   Be not alarmed at
the size of the catalogue.   What can not be accomplished in one year may in ten; nor are all histories to be
studied with equal care.   God, in his word, has epito-
mized the history of many generations, indicated the
chief points of attention in the field of later history—
the Assyrian, Medo-Persian, Grecian, and Roman—furnished in his providence the most able authors—Polyb-
ius, Livy, Thucydides, Xenophon, Rollin, Gibbon, etc.—
to illustrate them, and given us a clew to connect their
various parts and trace their important bearings.   We
may pass rapidly, by the aid of Hallam, through the
dark region of medieval history, and obtain imperfect
glances on the pages of Hume, Robertson, Russel, etc.,
of the more important events of modern times.   For
current history we need a well-edited daily, a weekly con-

densing its news, a monthly digesting the literature of the times, and a quarterly converging the mature thoughts of the passing age. Let us not spend too much time upon them; the periodical press is, to a great extent, trash; it caters for society, instead of elevating it; its miscellany is often weak and affected; its essays contentious, deceitful, superficial; its criticisms mere moths, fretting what they can not produce; its intelligence *chiefly* is to be valued. Nevertheless, it is indispensable: it lights up the world, though with gas; it circles the earth, though like the stars, in appearance only; it runs to and fro, though it does not always increase knowledge. There are, too, noble exceptions among editors—men whose essays are worthy to be studied as well for matter as style.

The history of human ideas or philosophy should be pondered. You have seen this tower of Babel at a distance; to mark its successive stories, to listen to the confusion of its tongues, and to trace its moss-grown ruins, is a task at once curious and profitable. Although no book is prepared for this purpose, yet we may extend our explorations by the light of such works as Enfield's or Brucker's. The acquisition of extensive and accurate knowledge of men and things of the past and present is indispensable, as well to a just appreciation of the best authors, as the proper employment of our own powers. It is thus we grow familiar with the muses, and make all nature vocal; thus we evoke Minerva from the brain, and give a harp to our sounding bowels. To philosophy let us add divinity. Concerning the relations of the soul to God, or life to immortality, we can know only what is revealed; for such knowledge it is vain to beat about in nature, or turn upon ourselves, for it is above both. Penetrated with this truth, we should come to the Bible with the docility of a child, and the awe of a prophet.

If you have received it as a revelation, it is too late to cavil, argue, or doubt, concerning it. You must receive a prophet in the name of a prophet if you would receive a prophet's reward. However humbling to the pride of reason may be this unquestioning belief, I enjoin it with the more confidence because you will accord it to something. You *will* seek rest in something infallible. "I am come in my Father's name, and ye receive me not; if another come in his own name, him ye will receive." Alas! there is as much difference between the revelations of Scripture concerning Divine things and the speculations of men, as between the solid world which Columbus discovered, and the dark, agitated, and liquid chaos which, beyond a certain horizon, presented itself to the imaginations of men before the days of that immortal navigator. And here let me advise you to read no skeptical works; they are unnecessary: a proposition and its contradictory need not both be investigated; if one be true, the other is false. You nave assented, after satisfactory proof and argumentation, to the truth of the Bible, and refuted the chief objections and arguments of infidels. What more is needed? The contradictory of the proposition may, however, be proved false directly, as well as indirectly, without any examination of infidel labors. It is nearly two thousand years since skeptics undertook to overthrow the Bible, and it is now more firmly, and intelligently, and extensively believed than ever. If the allies of the European west had been bombarding Sevastopol without intermission, with the progressive improvements in the art of war, for two thousand years, and yet found the fortifications of that port now ten times as strong as ever, you would conclude, without examining their parallels or batteries, that Sevastopol is impregnable. If infidelity finds the Bible a thousand times more firm after it has been arguing against it for eighteen hundred years, what will it find after it has argued in its most approved style for eighteen hundred years more?

We may take it for granted, that if it had one reliable argument it would in this wicked world be familiar as a household word. Moreover, the arguments of unbelievers are self-destructive; put them in parallel columns, and you may reduce them to zero by cancellation. Ancient infidels believed that Christ wrought miracles by the agency of devils; modern ones believe there is neither miracle nor devil.

If you read these works, they must produce either some effect upon your minds or none: if none, you lose your time and pains; if some, they must either shake your faith or overthrow it; if they merely shake it, they leave you a prey to doubt, which will distress you the more in proportion as you need rest of mind; if they overthrow your faith, they leave you exposed to universal skepticism concerning the past, impenetrable gloom concerning the future, and the wild play of the passions repressed only by very imperfect restraints.

Another object of reading is to keep the mind balanced. There are three great causes of mental maladjustment—the hand of nature, the lapse of time, and the pursuits of men. The college course has been wisely arranged to develop and train all the faculties; and although it does not correct all irregularities and make all minds symmetrical, it may, when properly pursued, prevent intellectual deformity. On leaving college we gradually undergo alterations: the sensibilities and the will gain upon the intellect; desire of action, power, money, fame, increases and rages, and in the conflicts of life we acquire a persistence, a firmness, a steadfastness, which we had not before exhibited: the intellectual states are also affected—imagination and memory lose power, abstraction and reason gain. Occupation will moaify these changes. As the foot of the Indian becomes fleet, and the eye of the sailor far-seeing, so the mind of the lawyer becomes acute, of the physician sagacious and practical, of the clergyman speculative and comprehensive. A discerning person can, at a glance, determine a man's profession, so deeply does it impress itself upon mind and manners. We should strive to prevent this daguerreotyping influence, and to secure a free movement for all our powers. Hence, if imagination begin to fail, read poetry; if business absorb the mind, study history till its characters, its events, its philosophy, arrest the attention and eclipse the trifles of the passing hour; if in the multitude of objects and amusements your mind is losing its concentrativeness, recur to mathematics, which, like a moral ladder, will keep you watchful as you ascend from round to round; if in the whirlpool of life you grow content with swimming superfices, return to the diving-bell of philosophy; and if in your association with the mass you become averse to ratiocination, and prone to take principles on trust, to leap to conclusions, and to argue *ad captandum*, go to the gymnasium of the schoolmen. There are, however, many works equally strengthening and more accessible than those of scholasticism: such as Chillingworth's defense of Protestantism, which it is said Daniel Webster read once a year to sharpen his logical skill; Fletcher's "Checks," of which a lawyer and an enemy said, "This argument will hold water;" Berkley's Minute Philosopher, which it is stated Robert Hall was accustomed to read regularly before he commenced that mighty and majestic movement of mind which often made his pulpit like unto Mount Sinai; Wesley's Sermons, as clear in logic as fervent in rhetoric, like the sea of mingled glass in apocalyptic vision—with lightning penetration he cleaves the forms of error till he reaches the reservoir of first truths, and, with a profound analysis, he not only guides you *into* the depths of pagan metaphysics, but *out* of them.

There are who object to this direction, and think that a man should concentrate all his powers upon his profession—if lawyer, he should let all his wisdom run to subtility; if poet, to fancy—and who look suspiciously on one who ventures beyond his ordinary range, as if he were doing injustice to his patrons. True, in order to shine we must converge our light; equally true, that we can not illustrate our own profession without ascending or *descending*, if you please, into others. We could not so easily survey a plain by walking continually within it as by ascending some eminence that overlooks it; nor could we form a just idea of the magnitude of a mountain without descending to the lower peaks. I believe in the communion of sciences as well as the communion of saints. It was the boast of Voltaire that he had discovered the island of England, so ignorant were his countrymen of its literature. There are many learned bodies to whom mathematics and poetry are unknown lands, and who think of law as good only for horse-thieves and physic for cutting off legs. Did the peculiar genius of the French cease to shine after they had been introduced to Bacon and Newton, and would gentlemen be less fitted to adorn one profession by some knowledge of another? Name a science to which any profession does not stand related or from which it may not draw illustrations and proofs. Name a man that has carried forward his profession who is not of general and varied reading and study. How did the Chinese become sluggish, or the monks of past ages mentally blind, but by shutting themselves up? How have some of the greatest philosophers become short-sighted by confining their attention to minute points? Be not a "Know-Nothing" in your profession, rather a "Know-Something" out of it; and remember that diverse knowledges may dwell together like soul and body. But what if your reading can not all be made tributary to your profession or pursuit? You have a higher mission—the cultivation of yourselves. He is narrow-minded, indeed, who will not visit a neighbor's hearth unless he can bake his own cakes upon its coals.

Another object of reading is to form the style. Works of rhetoric should be studied; but it is not by the philosophy of criticism that we can form a habit of writing felicitously. As by associating with gentlemen we acquire the manners of gentlemen, so by reading the best writers we attain to the art of good writing. "It is impossible," said Seneca, "to approach the light without deriving some faint coloring from it, or to remain long among precious odors without bearing away with us some portion of the fragrance." We shall more rapidly improve if we occasionally apply our rules of criticism, that by analyzing the beauties of the author we may more perfectly relish them, and by recognizing the principles upon which they are founded more readily reproduce them. Moreover, every author has his faults and imperfections, which we shall be liable to imitate, if we read without discrimination; indeed, so naturally do we transfer our admiration from excellences to blemishes associated with them, that we are as prone to imitate the *vices* as the *virtues* of a model. We should not confine ourselves to a single writer, however excellent he may be, lest he bore our ears through with an awl. Happily there is a great variety of master-pieces in composition. It is not our purpose to enumerate them. Suffer me to remark that, as a general rule, the older authors, who, writing before learning became widely diffused, addressed themselves to educated minds rather than the populace, such as Addison, Swift, Goldsmith, Pope, Cowper, and Young, are preferable; there are, however, recent writers whose style is beautiful, as Burke, Hall, Macaulay, Channing, Prescott, Irving. We should be guided in our selection by our peculiarity of genius—for each man has a peculiarity of intellectual character. Some men excel in the sententious style, others in the flowing; some are bold and figurative, others simple and delicate. If we are running our peculiarity to an extreme, we must check it by familiarity with a writer of opposite tendency. If you are too figurative, ponder Paley; if too terse, turn to Johnson; if wanting in energy, read Carlyle; if in purity, read Swift; if in elegance, Burke. After all, let us bear in mind that style is of *secondary* consideration. We should never run the risk of weakening our understanding or corrupting our principles for the sake of polishing our periods. I should fear to come within the fascinations of either Walter Scott or Dr. Channing. The more we think and feel, the less we need study style : an overflowing mind, like an overflowing river, will move gracefully ; a heart on fire, like a house on fire, will burn sublimely.

Another important object of reading is to stimulate the mind. Let me caution you against attempting to stimulate the intellect through the body in any other way than by taking care of your health. That the soul, like the embryo, is liable to be influenced by that in which it reposes is not denied, but the influence is a general one; the supposition that we can excite imagination by opium, memory by tea, or attention by whisky, as we can rouse the liver by calomel, or the nose by snuff, is a relic of ancient pathology, which located understanding in the brain, anger in the heart, and sensuality in the liver, and sought to purify the soul by purging the body. Yet some still seek to supply genius or atone for

idleness by a resort to stimulants and narcotics, pointing
to Lord Byron as an example; but if the bottle could
make poets the world would be full of them. It may
produce a temporary excitement, under the influence of
which men may compose rapidly that which they have
matured; and so of narcotics; but the compositions thus
produced are not of the highest order; they seem to be
the result of a wild and weird inspiration, such as
breathes in the Ancient Mariner of Coleridge and the
Raven of Poe. Like the henbane which infatuated the
ancient pythoness on her tripod, they produce a species
of moral convulsion suitable for divination and devil-
dealing, and should be reserved for the regions of magic
and superstition, or the age of ecstasies and dreams   If
you would have a clear, strong intellect, eschew them.
In the soul, as in the body, the law is deeply written:
"In the sweat of thy face shalt thou eat bread." Be
not deceived; truth is born only with travail; the spirit
is enfranchised only with agony. Nevertheless, there
are aids to the laboring soul. Is it sluggish, you may
rouse it: indirectly by a play of Shakspeare or a chapter
of Demosthenes; directly by a book of Milton or a page
of Ossian. In selecting for this purpose we must imitate
the discretion of the husbandman, who, having learned
the varieties of his soil, scatters ashes, lime, and manure,
and casts in the wheat, the barley, and the rye each in
its *appointed* time and place. To an imaginative mind,
imaginative works are the proper stimulants; to a ration-
ative, argumentative ones. If, being tasked, you would
excite your mind *at once*, turn to some choice collection
of stirring pieces—dramatic, senatorial, or martial—such
as start the soul like the tap of the reveille; and when
you have given "Hail Columbia" to your heart, give
your heart to the pen. But it is not enough to rouse the
soul; you must give it material; and there are works which

7

serve *this* purpose—products of original, profound thinking, and, like leviathans, few and easily distinguished, for they make the sea of thought around them boil like a pot. Some of these are as gas solidified; others as un-wrought gold; others like the hound that puts you upon the track of the game. The last are the most valuable; it is easy to let that which is compressed resume its original form or to mold the molten metal; it is more difficult and more healthful to pursue and overtake what has never been caught. Coleridge's Aids to Reflection is an example of the first kind; Butler's Analogy, of the second; Bacon's Advancement of Learning, of the third. Scarce a jar of modern metaphysical gas that has not been expanded from Coleridge; scarce a beautiful fabric of recent time on the evidences of Christianity for which Butler has not furnished the raw material; scarce a discovery in modern science since the days of James II to which Bacon has not pointed; and *yet* they can do more—the nature of the soil varies the crop even from the same seed. The deficiencies noted by Lord Verulam yet unsupplied are scores. All books that contain more than they express, that make the mind pause as it passes, that turn it back upon its own resources, or lead it on to new regions, are invaluable; they are educators; among ordinary books as Socrates among sophists. Most books are afraid to let the readers go alone a single yard, lest they dash their foot against a stone. Leave such to minds that need leading-strings. Seek books like unto blood-hounds, and hie to the chase : there are many such *absolutely*, though few, perhaps, will prove so *relatively* to all minds. Much depends on the reader's genius and habits; there are some men who can make almost any book suggestive, like the raven which, in dry weather, makes the scanty water rise to her beak by dropping pebbles into the hollow tree.

If we have a particular subject on hand, most well-written works on that subject will prove suggestive. In order to write orations, read orations; to write essays, read essays; only see that they are models, as Cicero and Addison. So if we have to write on a particular subject, as the atonement, we may read any strong work on it. Let us guard, however, against imitating the author; and this can be done by making a sketch upon the theme before we read upon it. This we shall not be likely to abandon; for a man loves a club-footed child of his own better than a perfect one of his neighbor's; and whatever thoughts occur to us, being used in our own order, and standing in new relations, are our own, as the waters of the Mississippi are no longer the Mississippi when in the bosom of the gulf. The most suggestive book in the world is the Bible. For thousands of years it has given activity and direction to the best portions of the world's mind. It has been during all this time the fountain of innumerable sermons and books, no two of which are alike; it is suggestive of trains of thought and rhetorical ornaments, of new themes and new arguments, of ever-purer emotions and ampler views; it is an everlasting feast of fat things—a tower, where the watchmen may observe the world's night and hail its morning—a Cas-talian fountain, fed from perpetual snows—a furnace, ever forging new and glowing forms of wisdom—a ceaseless orchestra of angels, lapping the soul in celestial music—a calm sunlight, consuming the vail that covers mortal eyes—a mountain raised between eternity and time, from whose summit we may look upon both. Above all, this is the book to accomplish the last great purpose of reading—the improvement of the heart, which I must dismiss with a word. I would not undervalue Taylor or Wesley, Gurnal or Baxter, Sherlock or Fuller, but if neither the Holy Living and Dying, the Saint's Rest, the Christian Armor, nor the Reformed Pastor, can move a cold heart, lay upon it live coals directly from the altar.

One word more.   Books are most suggestive and exciting in youth.   With you the soil is plowed and the clods broken; cast now the seed into the furrow, that, when the earth mourneth, and the vine languisheth, and the joy of the harp ceaseth, it shall not be as the shaking of an olive-tree or as the gleaning of grapes when the vintage is done; but that your barns may be filled with plenty, and your presses burst out with new wine The mind cultivated from youth puts on its noblest crown when the almond-tree flourishes, and enjoys a marvelous mental second sight when they that look out of the windows are darkened; judges have given their ablest decisions, physicians exhibited their highest skill, and divines produced their richest works, when the grasshopper was a burden

Hints to Youth.

WE hope that we have many young readers. For such we delight to write; because we may expect, without much vanity, to profit as well as to please them. Should grave wisdom direct its eye hither, we beseech it to turn over, while we endeavor to impart to youthful friends the benefit of our own experience and observation relative to certain small matters.

Take care of the *body*. It is a beautiful abode of the soul—all its apartments and furniture evince Divine wisdom and goodness—it is a system of useful instruments, by which the spirit may acquire knowledge and strength, and achieve works of wisdom and beneficence—it is a medium of communication with nature and with man—it is called, in Scripture, the temple of the Holy Ghost, and, in its incorruptible, spiritual, and glorious form, is to be the eternal habitation of the redeemed, and sanctified, and glorified soul. As we value the comfort and usefulness of the spirit, we should prize the health of the body—as we honor God, and admire his works, let us be careful of that beautiful specimen of his handiwork which he has committed to our keeping.

To secure the health of the body, it is necessary to exercise its members at least three hours a day. That employment or pastime is best which calls into exercise the greatest number of muscles.

But exercise, to be useful, must be taken with a good will, and in a good humor. A vigorous circulation re-

quires a cheerful heart, and an elastic footstep demands
a buoyant spirit.   Do not walk the street with a measured pace and downcast look, like a soldier marking time
to the "Dead March."   Don't work your problems, nor
mature your griefs, nor plan your enterprises in your
rambles.   But "over the hills and far away"—mount
Bucephalus, and, facing the morning sun, plunge into
the forest, and brush the dew from the bushes—or, calling your favorite dog, in the mellowed light of evening,
chase the fox, or tree the coon, or track the rabbit—or,
climbing the mountain-side, look out from its misty
brow—or sit by the cataract and commune with the dash-
ing waters, and scattering spray, and dancing rainbows,
and eternal murmurs—or chase the warbling rivulet,
and gaze on the beauteous forms mirrored in its clear
waters—or, if you please, look up cowslips on the mead-
ows, or poppies in the rye, or tulips in the valley for
your "Ain kin' dearie, O"—or, when in riper years,
run races with the little ones in the orchard, or through
the vineyards, or over the lawn.   Let your spirit learn
to be joyous in the fields of nature, and to catch the
inspiration of its light, and freshness, and green.   So
shall you have a merry pulse, a joyous arm, and a lively
footstep.

Inactivity is the temporal ruin of the man.   It brings
disease, cuts short the days, impairs the mind, disturbs
the temper, makes the subject and his companions miserable, and peoples fancy's airy world with a thousand hide-
ous forms.   Men are not always mindful that by indolence they induce disease.   No law of nature can be
violated with impunity; but because sentence against
lounging is not speedily executed, therefore the heart of
the sons of men is set in them to be idle.   Though the
sentence, however, be delayed, it is sure to come.   Justice may hobble along with a lame foot; but he will over-

take the sinner at last. You might as well hope to stop a race-horse on the brink of a precipice, as to avert disease if you fail to exercise the muscles. And when disease comes, no repentance or reformation shall seduce it from its work, though health be sought "carefully with tears."

Be as mindful, therefore, to take daily exercise as daily food. Do not say, "I have no time." To neglect the body is to lose time, by shortening your days. Do not say, "I will sacrifice my health to the improvement of my mind." You will find the mind rapidly fail under such a course. Whatever be your mental occupation, whether it demand memory, or fancy, or thought, or feeling, you can do more in five *minutes*, with a body renovated in the fields, and a mind inspired with nature's fairest works, than in five *hours*, under the influence of a sluggish pulse.

Would you be healthy, be careful in relation to your diet. As this is not a professional work, physiology would be out of place here. But suffer us to give a few plain directions, which we hope you will take upon trust when we assure you that they pass current with the doctors.

Though the appetite is the index to nature's wants, it is not always a true index. In disease it must often be disregarded, and in health it must never be fully satiated. Rise from breakfast *with* appetite, if you would not sit down to dinner *without* it. Ours is a land of abundance, and its inhabitants have acquired habits of indulgence unknown in many parts of the old world. If persons are abstemious they will rarely suffer from disease. The blood will course freely through the veins, the brain will sit at ease, and a feeling of comfort will spread over every organ and member. The intellect will feel at liberty, and bound with elastic step over the most diffi-cult steeps of science, or the most romantic fields of fancy. *Abstinence* is often of service, especially after indulgence. Was it not Bonaparte who said, "When my stomach gets out of humor, I withhold supplies till it cries for mercy?" Do not suppose that I would have you so abstemious as to induce feebleness. While the body would lose much, the soul would gain nothing from such a regimen. A vigorous intellect requires a healthy brain, and a cheerful brain demands a rich blood. If you eat to repletion, however, you sin, and must suffer. Under these circumstances, if you take proper exercise, your food may be digested; but the blood will be increased—its vessels enlarged—its circulation accelerated, and a state of plethora will be induced, which will render you liable to acute disease in various forms. But if you add indolence to gluttony, your digestive apparatus will fail under its accumulated labors, and dyspepsia, with all its crudities and acids, its melancholy apprehensions and sour spirits, will come upon you, rendering you a burden to yourselves and to others, and inducing your friends, perchance, to lock you up—in an editor's office.

In reference to the *quality* of food it matters but little, if the *quantity* be properly regulated. The stomach is an excellent chemist, and can analyze and compound almost any thing, if you do not give him too much to do. There are many things, however, placed on the table, which ought never to be seen there—such as pastry and preserves. If I had unlimited authority, I would banish them all. "But what should we do for dessert when favored with company?" Why, how much better is a plate of figs, or a basket of apples, or a few bunches of lucious grapes, than pies, cakes, or puddings? And as to liquids, cold water, milk and water, or lemonade, are far preferable to all the decoctions of foreign herbs. The former invigorate, the latter debilitate.

But I fancy a reader inquires, "Is the writer a Gra-

hamite?" By no means. We believe nature intended
that a man should have a mixed diet of animal and
vegetable food. We think anatomy and physiology, as
well as experience, teach this lesson. Nevertheless, we
humbly conceive that many countries—among them our
own—consume too much animal food. Perhaps, for
sedentary persons, animal food once a day is sufficient.

Be careful of your *personal appearance*. I do not ask
you to follow the fashions—to lay the neck bare one week,
and cover it with curly locks the next—to comb the hair
one way to-day and another way to-morrow; but I do ask
you to have as much mercy upon your own head as you
do upon your horse's; and while you direct the groom to
use the curry-comb, see that the barber uses the comb.
It has been said that cleanliness is next thing to godliness, and we have often wished that ablutions were a
part of our religion. We hope to see the day when the
bath-room shall be as common as the kitchen. We
think we shall then have cleaner prose, clearer music, and
sweeter poetry. The mind partakes in the comforts and
distresses of the body. O, for clear fountains and cool-
ing streams! Methinks they can almost put out the fire
of passion, and spread good nature through the soul.
Would you be in good humor with yourself, pay due
respect to your wash-stand. In cleanliness is seen one
of the great differences between the pagan and the
Christian. The sweetness of the sanctified spirit sheds
its influences upon the person.

Shall we be considered as descending if we allude to
apparel? We hate foppishness—aping great men. Because a prince, afflicted with king's evil, conceals his
neck in a high cravat, is that any reason why we should
bind up ours? Because some afflicted queen endeavors,
by the form of her dress, to hide a curvature of the
spine, why should the fair of America imitate her?

Extravagance in dress is as much to be condemned as foppishness. Let the ornaments of the man be a brilliant mind, a holy heart, and a meek and quiet spirit. Let the decorations of the woman be, not "pearls, or gold, or costly array," but modesty, intelligence, and sobriety. A Grecian matron, when asked for her ornaments, said, "The virtues of my husband are a sufficient ornament for me." Another, when challenged for her jewels, summoned her sons. It is proper, however, that our garments should comport with the habits of our country, and our pursuits and standing in society; and though comfortable, plain, and far from extravagant, they should evince a proper respect for ourselves and our fellow-men. We believe it is easier to go through the world in a good garment than in a ragged one; and as a man is responsible for all the influence he can acquire, he is bound to secure a decent apparel. "My banker," said one, "always makes a low bow to my *new* coat, and a slight one to my *old*." It will be time enough when we have mastered the world to disregard its prejudices. We pity the wife who is not as careful to please her husband as she was, when a maid, to please her beau.

Be mindful of your *manners*. True politeness is of great service. Its spring is good nature. One may, by reading books like Chesterfield's, and mingling in polished society, acquire certain habits, and obtain certain rules, which will enable him to pass off as a gentleman; but unless the milk of human kindness flows in his veins, and a just regard for his fellow-beings finds place in his heart, his politeness will be but disgusting hypocrisy. Vain is the attempt to deceive the world. It has too sharp an eye, and too thoughtful a brain. Every gesture and compliment is a matter of analysis, and through the most complicated processes of investigation is traced to its true motive. The great wor.d, too, is a good physi ognomist, and knows how to look through the window of the soul. To be polite is to please, but an *attempt* to please without the *desire* is worse than useless.

The best maxims of politeness are found in the Scriptures. Such are these: "Be kindly affectioned one to another with brotherly love, in honor preferring one another;" "Bear ye one another's burdens;" "Let no corrupt communication proceed out of your mouth, but that which is good to the use of edifying, that it may minister grace to the hearers;" "Wisdom is pure, peaceable, gentle, easy to be entreated, full of mercy and good fruits, without partiality and without hypocrisy;" "Charity vaunteth not itself, is not easily provoked, thinketh no evil," etc. Let that mind be in you which was in Christ Jesus, and you can not but be polite; for such a feeling will find expression in some form. Nature will be at no more loss to make it known than she is to give utterance to filial or maternal love; and however ungraceful or even offensive to ears polite may be the mode selected, the heart will acknowledge the language of its fellow-heart. Let a man, however, be endued with this feeling, and he can readily—by thoughtfulness and an observance of good models of gentility—acquire a graceful mode of expression. "Consider one another;" that is, think of your fellows, of their joys, their sorrows, their hopes, their disappointments, their interests—think how you can allay their griefs, or promote their happiness—think of your friends, and of what you would do and say under an exchange of circumstances. It may be that the kindest men may be deemed boorish, at times, for want of consideration. Would you learn gentility, observe those who have it.

Be careful of your *temper*. A glad heart makes a sweet countenance, and a smiling face is like the sun in his beauty. Whatever may be the attraction of a lady's

intellect, or person, or acquirements, she is **repulsive, if**
she be of a gloomy disposition. Her best friends will
be uneasy in her presence; and though some "good
Samaritan" may be willing to pour oil upon her wounded
spirit, the priest and the Levite will instinctively pass
by on the other side. We have generally sorrows enough
of our own, without hearing one another's woes. Most
of our troubles are imaginary. Never, therefore, nurse
evil apprehensions, and you will never be melancholy.
There is no philosophy like the philosophy of the Scriptures: "Take no thought for the morrow: sufficient unto
the day is the evil thereof." Were every one satisfied
with her daily bread of affliction, there would be but
little murmuring. Keep in good humor with the future—
it has never done you harm—why complain of it? Bear
kindly the afflicting dispensations of Providence. They
are all arranged for your good; and if cheerfully and
piously endured, will be pleasing and profitable exercises
for the heart or mind, or both. Providence, moreover,
like the earth, is in perpetual revolution, and its darkest
midnight is followed by the dawn. There is a heavenly
alchemy which transmutes anguish into rapture. I would
oppose to Pandora's Box, Paul's paradox—"As sorrowful,
yet always rejoicing." David's heart caroled in its sad-
ness, and the wildest and sweetest notes of his harp were
touched by the hand that felt the Father's rod. Why
should a living man complain? When stripped of every
thing, bow down in humble and grateful adoration, and
thank God that you have a body and a soul. And shall
a saint repine? Would a pardoned culprit, trembling
beneath the halter, complain because the government did
not send a coach and four to convey him from the gal-
lows? and shall a sinner, raised from the mouth of hell,
murmur because angel wings don't waft him *gently* to
the throne of God?

A melancholy mind imparts a gloomy tinge to every thing around it. Though nature, to the clear eye, is like to Eden, yet for the jaundiced one she has no charms. No hills are green—no dells are dewy—no paths are flowery—no steeps are breezy to moping grief. In Providence there is a bright and a dark side to every picture. Endeavor to look constantly at the latter. He who searches for trouble is pretty sure to find it—he who courts enjoyment sees her not afar.

Always keep in good humor with *yourself*. We would not have you blind to your sins, but know the worst of them, and repent and believe to the saving of the soul But be satisfied with your capacities of mind and body. Rest assured they are the best for you—the very gifts which Infinite Wisdom sees that you can best improve. Be satisfied with your sphere. Sometimes you will meet with disappointments—**bear** them with grace. For instance, you intend to be a speaker—well, beware of mortification. You read, and study, and write, and intend to make a wonderful display—you expect now to raise a shout, and now a laugh, and now, perchance you hope to see a lady faint; and anon you design to raise the audience to their feet; and you promise yourself that, as you leave the court-room, every eye will look toward you, and the young ladies will smile, and become envious of the favorite; and she, the beloved of the orator, will be entranced, and murmurs of applause will roll in whispers on your ear, such as "great man," "fine speech," "true eloquence." The day arrives—the audience assemble—all eyes are fixed—all ears are open—handkerchiefs rise up to catch the tears, and smelling-bottles push their corks half open. The speaker labors—alas! his mind is rigid—his tongue is stiff—his figures flounder—his arguments tumble down—the peroration is forgotten. The audience rise in confusion, and the speaker sits down in perspiration. And now the ladies smile at one another, the favorite hides her head, and the young rivals sneer, and the malicious breezes whisper, "Rather flat."

Well, young man, hold up your head. Do not let the audience know that you have failed, and they will, perhaps, soon forget the failure, or even change their minds, and reproach their dullness for not perceiving your brilliancy, and their shallowness for not appreciating your profundity. Suppose you have failed, and every body knows it. Do not be troubled—calm yourself with the consolation of the valorous Falstaff—"He that fights and runs away, may live to fight another day."

Keep in a good humor with the world. Mankind are not all rascals, though an honest man wants bread. The world are not all fools, though a genius has no praise. Remember that Homer sung for bread, and Goldsmith wrote in a garret; and who are you? You may be great and wise—we do not dispute your claims—you may be a Cicero or a Webster—a Mrs. Sigourney or a Hannah More; but you must give the world a fair opportunity to understand your powers. Moreover, you may make the world as cross or good-natured as you please. If you treat it roughly, you will be treated roughly in return. Smile at it, and it will answer with a smile. He that would have friends, must show himself friendly. Do not look round for imperfections, saying, here is a rascal, and there is a fop, this is a fool and that is a bankrupt. It may all be true; but why say so? *Cui bono?* Look round for excellences. If you contend with the world you will find fearful odds against you Speak evil of no man. When others speak evil of a man, do you speak good. No man so perfect as not to have some defects-- none so frail as not to have some fine quality.

And now my pen addresses itself particularly to the

young gentlemen. Be in the good graces of the ladies. You have learned already that a mother's love, though cheap, is priceless—that a sister's affection is an impenetrable shield. I pity the youth who does not know the value of woman's influence. He can not succeed Whether he be carpenter or mason, sovereign or shoeblack, priest or politician, he is a ruined man without the favor of the ladies. No pursuit so low, none so high, as to be beyond woman's reach. Needles and bayonets move at her command—turkeys and tyrants roast on her spit—coursers and candidates run at her will, and crowds and cradles hush at her lullaby. Her smile is prosperity—her indignation brings trouble. Great as is her influence, it is no more than she deserves. The purest feelings of the heart receive their earliest and noblest developments in her character. The mother's affection, the wife's devotion, the sister's love, who shall paint? In scenes of poverty and suffering she is an angel of mercy. At the altar of God her prayers are the warmest incense, her songs the sweetest praise.

But how shall woman's influence be secured? The weak side of a mother's heart is her maternal love. You may easily procure a welcome to the family if you treat the children with kindness and attention. Notice the babe—its blue eye—its rosy cheek—calm its griefs, and enter into its tiny joys. And who would not? Are you the man, reader? Then there is no love nor music in your soul, and you do not deserve favor. What creature so beautiful as the infant man? Our Savior took little children in his arms and blessed them.

Make the best of your country and location. The foreigner generally brings down a world of prejudices upon himself by contrasting his native with his adopted country. Comparing Washington with London, the White House with Windsor Castle, Trinity with St. Paul's, he disgusts all around him. Give him an apple, **and he** must speak of the superior orchards of Great Britain, **or** a peach, and he will boast of the size and flavor of those across the water. Present him a basket of cherries, and he praises the large, luscious English garden cherry, that grows by the wall. He meets with nothing to please him—as though we had no earth or heaven, water or atmosphere, thunder or lightning, worth a farthing. Were he to turn his attention and conversation upon our advantages, upon the superiority of our forests and mountains, our seas and rivers, our soil and climate, he would receive a hearty welcome, and be a popular man.

We have known a talented and pious clergyman to lose all influence with his people by harping on the evils and disadvantages of his location, while we have seen his inferior become a universal favorite by pointing out the beauties and excellences of the surrounding hills.

Beware of bad *habits.*

"Choose that which is most fit," said Pythagoras, "and custom will make it most convenient." There are many bad habits prevalent in our day of which we would have you beware. Gentlemen have a fashion of *sitting* which we know must give ladies much uneasiness, since it wears holes both in the carpet and the wall, and often divorces the seats of chairs from their backs. A worthy and witty friend propelled us to the borders of convulsions once. at his hospitable table, when he described the predicament, on a particular occasion, of a certain individual, who, having perhaps read in Thomas Aquinas, that the human intelligence rocked itself on the center of two horizons, was in the habit of reminding himself of that sublime truth, by poising his body upon his chair. On a visit to President Jefferson, being somewhat embarrassed, and not paying due respect to his antero-posterior motions, he was very painfully assured of the important

princip.e that bodies corresponding solely to time and
space, have both a *hic* and a *nunc*, so that if by gravita-
tion or any other cause they are removed from one place
they must go to another. We can think of no excuse for
the habit to which we refer, unless the philosophy be
correct which teaches that to attain to true wisdom a man
must imitate the motion of the stars, so as to produce a
giddiness which frees the mind from "sensible notions,"
and raises it to the region of illumination. In spite of
Tophail, however, the ladies can cure this habit at once
by having castors put under their chairs.

There is a plant which was hailed, at its introduction
into the world, in the middle of the fifteenth century, as
one of the wonders of America, and which, through a
strange coincidence, was first conveyed into the eternal
city by a descendant of that illustrious man who first
brought to Rome the wood of the true (?) cross. This
plant appears to have a peculiar charm for three animals:
a certain worm, a particular goat, and a creature in the
image of God. It is used in various forms: some grind
it to powder, and offer it to themselves as the heathen
present incense to their idols—others curl it into little
stems which they burn, as the converted pagan does his
god; while a third class roll it, like the sinner does his
sins, as a sweet morsel under the tongue. We protest, *ex
cathedra*, against its use in any form.

The practice of using *snuff*—not uncommon among the
fair—injures the voice. We have known several distinguished speakers deprived—in no small degree—of their
charm by this habit. Nor is this the worst. Why did
Pope Urban VIII publish a decree of excommunication
against all who took snuff in the Church? Though we
grant that this bull was rather severe, we believe, nevertheless, that his Holiness was a very discerning man.

The practice of *smoking* causes a waste of time and

money, and subjects us to great inconvenience. A man
will sometimes find company, even at his own fireside, to
whom the ashes and fumes of tobacco are far from agree
able.   I speak not now of such as are peculiarly suscepti-
ble, and liable to "die of a rose in aromatic pain." Very
few who have not been accustomed to breathe such incense as that of the pipe, can endure it long in a close
room without discomfort.   And what will you do, gentle
reader, if you become the room-mate—at college or else-
where—of one whose olfactories and lungs are delicate,
or when shut up in a stage-coach or a cabin on a cold
day, with nervous companions, to whom you are bound to
show respect?   Should you carry this habit into the itin-
erant ministry, how often will it give you uneasiness!
You will not, surely, defile the *prophets'* chamber, or the
holy altar.

This practice offends against what has been called—
next thing to godliness. We would not declaim against
it as did King James I, who said it was "a custom loathsome to the eye, hateful to the nose, harmful to the brain,
dangerous to the lungs, and in the black stinking fumes
thereof nearest resembling the horrible Stygian smoke
of the pit that is bottomless;" but we may surely be allowed to say that it is not charming to the senses.   We
have seen ladies smoking—young ones, too. O, tell it
not in Christendom; publish it not in the streets of Cincinnati!   It was customary among the ancients for a lass
to eat a quince on her bridal day, that her breath might
be fragrant at the altar, and that the odor of her lips
might suggest mellifluous discourse, and spiritual sweetness.   What bridegroom would not prefer the odor of the
quince and its purifying associations, to the fumes of the
"herb of immortal fame," and dreams of bar-rooms and
blackguards?

We know it is unpopular to write against a favorite

custom; but then we do not, as did the legislature of Russia in 1634, forbid your smoking, under pain of having your noses cut off, nor do we propose to issue a decree, as did Amurath IV, pronouncing it a capital offense. We write so gently that you can not be offended; indeed, when we see a man in the winter of life sitting by a lone fire, and musing over the flight of happy hours, we would not diminish the consolation which he draws, in his solitude, from his long white pipe tipped with red sealing wax; nor would we deprive the rude Indian of his emblem of peace, nor the slave of his socializer, nor the wandering Arab, or the hardy Esquimaux, of a luxury which sweetens his bitter hours; but we advise the young, and such especially as dwell within the precincts of civilized life, to seek for solace of a different kind.

We have not spoken of the *other form of using tobacco;* but as that is so disgusting, we will presume none of our readers are addicted to it; nor need we tell the story of Mrs. S., who spread out her beautiful white satin apron before her guests, as they were defiling her new Brussels carpet, saying, "Use this, gentlemen; I can wash this, but not my carpet." Allow us, in conclusion, to say that tobacco, in any form, is ordinarily injurious to health. We do not, however, wish to deprive the steam doctors of it, nor speak disparagingly of its merits; it is a good emetic.

We should not have touched upon this plant, but for the fear that its popularity is increasing, and that it has a great tendency to produce intemperance by causing a dryness of the *fauces,* for which a remedy is too often sought in the glass.

Avoid the habit of *speaking carelessly,* using ungrammatical expressions, low phrases, unauthorized words, provincialisms, etc. This, you will say, is a very small matter; but if a neglect of such counsel should preclude your admission into more refined circles of society, it will prove to you a matter of some consequence. Wealth, station, influential connections, may do much toward securing respect; but vulgarity can counteract them all. Wit and intelligence, enchanting as they are, can not atone for those coarse expressions which denote ill-breeding and low conceptions. Many amiable ladies, whose connections are wealthy, of high official standing, and great political influence, wonder why it is they are not admitted to the circles to which they aspire. Not a few of this class could solve the perplexing problem which imbitters their existence, if they would pause over the hint just given. Pedantry and affectation are as much to be avoided as vulgarity. A pretended delicacy of expression is often a sign of real indelicacy of thought. Words are often corrupted by the channel through which they pass. To the pure all things are pure: *"Honi soit qui mal y pense."* We question the refinement which calls Hog Island Swine Island, and dog the "domestic quadruped which guards the habitation." The language of Paris is that of attenuated refinement; yet it is the vehicle of the grossest moral pollution. Above all, shun every appearance of *profanity*. It is a sure sign of very bad breeding or a very bad heart. Was it not the prince of modern philosophers who took off his hat when he passed a church? Is it not said of Boyle that when he pronounced the name of Deity he uncovered his head? How often is the title of Jehovah—that name which rends mountains—the tower of the persecuted Christian—the hope of the dying man—the name at which heaven bows, earth shakes, hell trembles—used with as little regard as that of a slave!

Violate not the first commandment: better kiss the cannon's mouth. How deep the depravity that can trifle with the name of the Creator! For other sins an excuse may be pleaded; for there is scarce any which does not confer or promise pleasure for a season. This sin can point to no part of our nature, and say to the inquiring Judge, "The passion which thou gavest me did tempt me, and I did eat." It is the development of sheer depravity, unless the transgressor can plead that he has come up from the very dregs of society, where there is no other dialect but that of hell. When at Washington City, I heard it said of one high in office, "He swears even in the presence of ladies." I trembled and I hoped. I saw that the nation was defying Heaven: I saw, also, that religion was not yet driven from her stronghold—woman's heart. To the honor of woman, let it be said, that to swear in her presence is the climax of impoliteness.

Be careful of your *character*. No youth can succeed in the world without a good reputation. A man may have genius, and fancy, and wit—profound learning—a charming person—a sparkling conversation; and yet, devoid of integrity, who will give him employment, or bid him welcome? We may admire him; but only as we do a beautiful and dangerous beast. The shepherd may smile at the tiger bounding through the forest, or reposing in his den; but he would shudder to see him among the lambs of his flock. To obtain good character we must have good morals. I need not say there is no morality like that of the Scriptures. Keep the ten commandments—they are of infinitely more value than the morals of Seneca, the precepts of Socrates, or the Lives of Plutarch. They are radiant with heavenly light, and worthy of God. He who observes them occupies an elevated post in the moral world. He enjoys the approbation of his reason, his conscience, and his heart—he commends himself to sinner no less than saint—he is blessed of God. Earth rejoices before him, and joy unbidden dances in his heart. I know there appears to be no just hand in this life to distribute good and evil according to desert; yet the observation of all men will justify the remark, that integrity is indispensable to permanent prosperity. Though the immoral man may succeed for a time, he shall not prosper long. Reason will weaken him with her reproaches, conscience alarm him with her terrors, and the divine curse overtake his footsteps.

Would you understand the commandments, however, bring them to the Sermon on the Mount. In the light of this commentary, we see their beauty and divinity. They are not confined to the overt act; they require a sinless motive. Would you keep the commandments perfectly, you must not have a heart from which proceed "evil thoughts, murders, adulteries," etc. I know there is an outside morality, which makes a man as a whited sepulcher; but trust it not; the stone may be rolled away, and the rottenness laid open to the light of heaven. Would you have perfect, and pure, and vital morality, you must have a purified heart. Make the fountain pure, and the stream will be pure. But where shall the heart be washed of its stains? In the fountain of a Savior's blood. I have no faith in any morality that has not found out "Jesus Christ and him crucified."

These general observations are sufficient for our purpose; but I can not refrain from some specific directions. Be observant of truth. Scarce any man falls into vice and crime who is willing, at all hours, to tell the truth, the whole truth, and nothing but the truth. Falsehood is the gate of the road to ruin. If once a young man learns to lie, he is ready for almost any sin; because he fancies he has found a method of concealment. Who steals, who counterfeits, before he has learned to falsify? Hence, Satan is called the father of lies. "All liars are

'o have their portion in the lake that burneth with brim-
stone." An intuitive perception of the guilt of falsehood
makes the appellation "liar" exceedingly offensive. Make
no distinction between white and black lies. Beware of
allowing gesticulation, or manner, or countenance, to
falsify. Remember that you may lie without speaking,
that you may lie by exaggerating, or diminishing the
truth; that you may lie even *with* the truth, by giving it
a wrong arrangement.

Be cautious how you make promises; make none which
you do not intend to fulfill. I know that such directions
are not suited to our times of reckless trading and wild
speculation. I am aware, too, that such care and caution
may be incompatible with rapid accumulation; but I
know, also, that the steps of one who pursues such a
course, though slow, are sure; and when he gains the
summit, he does not find it crumble beneath him. How
immense the advantages of a man who, having acquired a
reputation for punctuality, passes his promises as silver!
How easy for him to command capital or secure patron-
age! Many are not aware that the habit of falsifying
steals on insidiously. We first lie for amusement, then
for convenience, next to conceal guilt, or gratify malice,
till, finally, we can bear false witness against our neighbor, without the least compunction. Beware, then, of
the smallest beginnings of falsehood. Be guarded in
speaking of *motives* or matters of *opinion*, remembering
that he who asserts any thing as true, assumes the responsibility of ascertaining it to be so.

Consider the dangerous consequences of falsehood.
The fortune and character which had been acquired by
a long life of usefulness, has often been blasted by a single
falsehood. A soul has not unfrequently been hurled to
ruin by one lie. Witness Ananias and Sapphira. Tell
me not that lying is essential in your profession or trade.

It is a libel on divine Providence. There is no lawful pursuit in which truth is not far more advantageous than falsehood. The obligations to speak the truth, and the blessings which flow from it, do not depend upon the pursuits of the speaker, or the rights of the hearer, but our relations to God. Truth is lovely in herself. Learn to venerate her as the leader of virtue, the mother of science, and the attribute of God.

With a view to facilitate an observance of truth, I subjoin a few cautions. Be slow in making promises. As much as lieth in you, owe no man any thing but love. Be wary how you borrow or lend. The practice of promiscuous borrowing is a great fountain of falsehood and misfortune. I will not say that we ought never to lend. The great father of English poetry says, without qualification, "Neither a lender nor borrower be;" and, perhaps, if a man were to consider his own interest only, this would be an unexceptionable precept; for, as the great dramatist says, "Use doth oft destroy both itself and friend."

But we are not to look *solely* to our own interest; and higher authority than Shakspeare informs us that it is our duty to lend to the poor. We are rarely, however, under obligation to borrow; suffer rather than do so. Better go barefoot and bleeding over the ground than run the risk of losing a friend, blunting conscience, and incurring self-degradation, by borrowing means to buy shoes. Don't tell me about the necessity of borrowing. Few men not possessed of considerable resources can do so without plunging into a whirlpool of engagements from which it is difficult to get out with a clear character and conscience.

Be decided, not only in your opinions, but your course of action. Having chosen your path from a conviction of its rectitude, suffer nothing to divert you. Rather starve, or bleed, or burn, than act contrary to the convictions of your judgment. The desire to please is an amiable trait in the character of youth, and is often confounded with humility and modesty; but it is different from either, and has been the temporal and eternal ruin of thousands.

Firmness is the helm of the mind. It can direct a feeble intellect across a stormy ocean. Without it, no force of thought, no depth of feeling, no resources of .earning, no power of eloquence, no clearness of mental vision, is safe upon the voyage of life. Splendid abilities deprived of its guidance, are destined to be but a splendid wreck. It is an indispensable element in the character of the good man. To be virtuous in the midst of wickedness, is to be singular. He who follows the multitude in this world must do evil. The man who passes through the wide gate, and down the broad way, goes to destruction. What would Daniel have been without firmness? One of the precepts of the Gospel is, "Be ye steadfast, immovable." The rock in the midst of the sea, which, in the stormiest as well as the calmest hour, lifts its venerable head above the billows, is the best emblem of the Christian.

Firmness is not eccentricity. The former is founded in regard for one's own opinions; the latter in contempt for those of others. Firmness is singular in matters of importance; eccentricity is singular at all times. Who had more firmness than Paul; and yet who, in trivial matters, was more accommodating? Though he everywhere held up the cross, yet, on Mars' hill, he paid respect to philosophy; and, in Jerusalem, he honored Moses. In condescension to the Greek, he refrained from meat, and, to please the Jew, he circumcised Timothy. Steadily keeping salvation in view, he was "all things to all men."

Firmness is not obstinacy. The former rests upon

reason, the latter upon will. The former implies intelligence, the other stupidity. The one is a high excellency,
the other a great defect. The one is illustrated in Luther
standing before the Diet of Worms, the other in the mule
standing under the lash of his master.

Be careful *in relation to your company.* Some of you
may be about to leave the circle of your family, and the
companions and guardians of your youth; but, as man
was formed for society, you will soon find other associates.
Beware : extend your confidence slowly; and, while you
treat *all* with respect, be careful how you admit *any* to
the endearing relation of friend. If you look over the
history of the past, or the scenes of the present, you will
see two classes of men : the one advancing to honor and
happiness, the other plunging into infamy and ruin. And
what accounts for the difference? The respective character of their early companions. "Be not deceived—evil
communications corrupt good manners." Avoid infidel
associates. You have been born of pious parents, and
reared under holy influences. The very gambols of your
boyhood have been among the green pastures, and beside
the still waters of the Shepherd of souls. You have seen,
upon your native mountains, the beautiful feet of Him
"that bringeth good tidings—that publisheth peace."
You have heard, with infant ears, "the joyful sound"
that makes the people blessed. You have breathed a
moral atmosphere, purified with the dews of the Gospel.
You have gone up to the temple to worship, and, with
infant voices, have caroled Jehovah's praise. Perhaps,
reader, you are a *Peter* called from his net to be a fisher
of men; and by your side is a *David,* invited from the
mountains of Bethlehem to the throne of Israel; and here
is one on whom, while looking into heaven, the mantle of
an Elijah hath fallen ; and there is the son of some
Hannah, a child of vows and tears, dedicated to God in

his temple, by her whose trembling heart said, "So long as he liveth he shall be lent to the Lord." Here is that Samuel who, when the word of the Lord was precious, as he lay by the ark of God, said, "Speak, Lord, for thy servant heareth."

But you are about to leave the paths of youth and go down into the wilderness. Beware! I am not afraid that you will seek companions in the bar-rooms, and in the corners of the streets. You *shudder* at the blasphemies of those cruel scorners who can hurl down, with malignant pleasure, the poor souls whom they allure to the dark mountains of unbelief, and look with mad indifference upon the eternal ruin of the victims whom they betray to the hands of Satan. You will not listen, while the Bible, and the blood which speaketh mercy, and the temple, which lifts its vail from the counsels of the eternal Mind, are reviled. But you should remember that there is a *refined* infidelity. You will meet with young men of engaging manners, cultivated minds, and elegant attainments, whose thoughts and feelings are tinctured with skepticism. These men know how to insnare you. Praising the poetry of Isaiah, the morality of the Gospel, and the character of Jesus, they will treat your religion with respect, and go to the house of God in your company. But, at the same time, they will give you to understand that they see excellences in the Koran and the Talmud, as well as the Bible; that they venerate the son of Sophroniscus as well as the Son of Mary, and that they have a similar regard for the Arabian kneeling at the tomb of the prophet, or the Brahmin prostrate at the feet of his idol, that they entertain for you at the supper of the Lord. Descanting upon the prejudices of early education, and the power of custom, and sneering at enthusiasm and superstition in all their forms, they will ingeniously turn the contempt they arouse against these, her accidental concomitants, upon the holy religion which they deform. While they raise a cloud before your eyes, which hides God from your view, they will steal into your doubting heart, robbing it of all faith in God's word, all hope in his mercy, all traces of his love; and leaving you in a world of wickedness and misery, without any support for your virtue, any consolation for your woe, or any hope in a better world! Alas! what may we expect will be your career? and in what manner will it close? Who shall help you on your dying pillow, when the terrors of the grave rise, and the curtains of despair fall, and the furies of remorse wake up, and hell opens its mouth for the lost soul? O, Jesus, may we never leave thy cross! Shun the most splendid society if it be of infidel tendency. No accomplishment so elegant, no learning so profound, no honor so resplendent, as to compensate the child of God for the least seed of doubt that skepticism can plant in his heart.

Avoid the company of the gay or dissolute. Far be it from me to recommend austerity or gloom. There is nothing in my philosophy or my feelings which would rob youth of one of its rational pleasures. There is useful mirth as well as salutary woe. And it becomes us all to sit down to life's feast with pleasure, and rise from it with gratitude But let your pleasures be *rational*, not sensual—the pleasures of *man*, not those of the *brute*. Let the feast be the feast of *reason*, and the wine the flow of *soul*. Immortal mind should need no material stimulant As iron sharpeneth iron, so the face of man his friend.

While mind struggles with mind, and heart bounds to heart—while thought leaps out to thought, and joy dances to joy—while mutual sympathy hightens mutual rapture—there are hights and depths of pleasure never known to the cockpit, the race-course, or the ball-room.

Although the habits of the age are temperate, yet there

are a thousand avenues to the drunkard's grave. On the steamboat and on the street, in the city and in the field, there are those who "lie in wait to destroy." Hundreds are ready to lead you to the card-table, and from the card-table to the wine-cup, and thence to the scenes of alluring vice, where pleasure decks her bowers, and spreads her bed of poppies, and, in the words of the poet, "weaves the winding-sheet of souls, and lays them in the urn of everlasting death."

Be careful of your *mind*. *Inform* it. There is as clear evidence that the mind was made to learn as that the feet were made to walk. All nature is hung with leaves of instruction, and a flood of light spreads over them to make their lessons luminous. The Bible is a book from heaven, ample in its evidence, sublime in its revelations, clear and copious in its instructions, pure in its precepts, rich and precious in its promises. Above all, there is a divine light which beams upon the humble soul. These three sources of knowledge are exhaustless and pure. Commune much, then, with nature, with revelation, and with God. Beware of other sources of knowledge. We fear both men and books. Granted, that *holy* men are good counselors, religious books helps to wisdom. Try both by the divine oracles. If they speak not according to this, there is no light in them. Books of history, of geography, and of true science, are but transcripts of Providence and nature. Of these we need not be fearful; but works of human genius are to be suspected. The memory is an immortal canvas, and the forms traced upon it will probably be enduring as God. Beware whose brush you suffer to approach it. Thought may be buried, but the hour cometh when it shall have a resurrection, and be hung up in eternal light to the gaze of men and angels. Moreover, there is a Mind so pure that the heavens are not clean in his sight—so transcendent that he charges his angels with folly; and that mind searcheth hourly the heart. Let us beware whose inkhorn we let down into the bosom.

Though an impure thought may give a moment's amusement, it may afterward cost unspeakable anguish. Who shall tell the torment of that spirit, when, in the hour of its painful trial, the infidel doubt which it received in the days of its wickedness, rises like a lost spirit from the pit, to haunt it through the darkness? Novelist, there cometh an hour when death shall seize. Then every stanza of Zion, and every verse of the Bible, will be an angel to thy soul. But, alas! the impure thoughts of Shakspeare, and Byron, and Butler, may be commissioned, like horrid specters, to drive you away from hopes of mercy, and promises of God, into the very terrors of hell. In that sad moment of despair, what would you give for a rod to drive away the ghosts of impurity and sin that hover round thy dying pillow?

Consider. Let all you learn be subjected to examination, fair and full. Read, then meditate, understand, appropriate. Keep a sentinel at the door of the mind, charged to admit no stranger who does not give the countersign. When any important fact comes into your presence, survey it carefully: inquire into its nature, its origin, its uses, and how to make it bear upon your object. He who perpetually reads, but never inquires, is like a stranger in the midst of a mob—he knows not friend from foe, nor which way to flee to escape danger.

In the economy of God, high achievement issues only from commanding mind; commanding intellect can only be brought forth by painful mental travail. *Control* the mind. Magnificent are its powers immortal; glorious the improvement, or terrible the havoc, which they must make in the universe; high and luminous the elevation, or dark and profound the abyss which must follow its labors, according as they are well or ill-regulated. You can do much to acquire command of your powers, by long and laborious exertion. The reason can be trained to patient, powerful, consecutive thought—but not without a will, which to the soul is as the voice of God to the universe. To think, in this world of sights and sounds, and fragrance and sweets—of fancies and follies, cares and duties—is no easy task. Ulysses, as he passed the rock of the Siren, stuffed the ears of his companions with wax, and lashed his own body to the mast. He who would escape the rocks of folly, as he sails deep seas of thought, must learn to shut the gates of the senses, and bind his intellect with strong cords. The imagination is of incalculable value, but it needs to be under stern control. It is a beautiful world of dreams, in which the soul may advantageously luxuriate—dancing through its castles, communing with its heroes, imparadising itself in its bowers, and returning to the real world with the motion, the beauty, the fragrance, and the song of an angel fresh from the scenes of light. But we must be careful not to tarry too long in our visits to those enchanting regions—not to forget that we are visitors there, that our proper sphere is the world of matter—let us always maintain a proper command of the ivory gate, so that we may at once and always have free egress to the upper air.

The passions are a vast deep; it is good this deep should oft be moved. Let the east wind, and the north, and the south, and the west, bursting from their caves, together meet upon its waters; let the waves rise and the sands be thrown up, and the spray sprinkle the stars, and heaven and earth be commingled; but take care that there shall always be a Neptune within the soul, to raise his calm head above the billows, and driving the struggling winds to their strong prisons, and calming the troubled waters, make a tranquil surface on which to retreat to his ocean home.

I tremble, reader, to think that you are plunged into the depths of the universe, with an immortal soul, responsible to a holy and infinite God. Let constant prayer ascend, that the Holy Spirit may never "leave you alone."

Finally, save your soul. What gain can compensate for its loss? Who, that reads his own heart in the light of God's law, does not feel guilty? There is mercy and there is wrath in Jehovah—to which of them shall the sinner be consigned? Jesus Christ is wisdom, righteousness, sanctification, and redemption. Up, dying sinner, to his cross!